THE SORCERER'S ABSOLUTION

BOOK 2 OF THE DRAGON KEEPERS SERIES

JESSICA KEMERY

HOT MESS
EXPRESS PUBLISHING

Cover: **Covers by Christian**

Editing by: Ashley Smith-Roberts

Proofreading by: Horus Copyedit and Proofreading

Formatting: Hotmessexpresspublishing.com

ISBN: 979-8351111537

CONTENTS

MAP

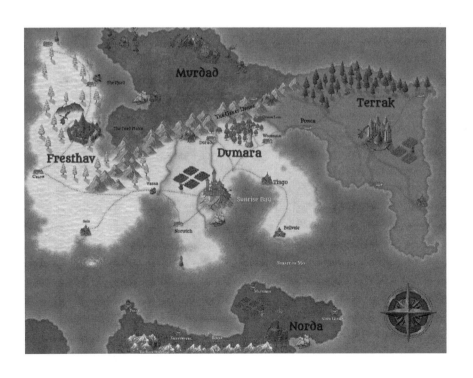

CHAPTER 1

DRAGON EGGS

The dragon, huge and hulking, loomed over the smaller dragon. His pale yellow sides heaved with anger, and a low growl emanated from the back of this throat. Torrid, a warrior with the sunrise clan, looked at the smaller dragon with pure malice. His voice was merely a hiss and drool dripped from his fearsome fangs. "You are a travesty. You have been nothing but trouble since you brought that summer dragon home. You and your wife spread divisiveness among the clan. I'm warning you, Nick, shut up all your little friends, or there will be consequences. I don't care if you are a Prince of Dumara."

Nick Chuvash, in his dragon form, was pure red with a golden streak down his back. He had a short golden mane and, like the rest of the royal family, piercing blue eyes. "How dare you speak to me like that!" he roared, puffing his chest out. "I do not spread divisiveness. I have gathered the small, the lame, the outcasts, and you and my brother would do well to listen to them. But my brother is only interested in mating recently, isn't he?"

Torrid had enough. With a mighty roar, he swiped at the Prince, rising on his hind legs. With his massive body, he pushed into Nick, forcing him back into the wall of the cave. It was the ultimate show of domination, and no one but Torrid would dare use this technique on a Prince of Dumara. "Do not speak of your brother and my daughter like that! Your brother Alex is the Crown Prince, and he is one hundred times the dragon you are, you cowardly little cuss. Now, remove yourself from my sight before I do something I regret," he roared, and light rays flew from his mouth, striking a glancing blow to Nick's hindquarters. With a whimper and a squeal, Nick retreated down the corridor without looking back.

Torrid glared at him in anger, slowly calming himself. No one spoke badly of his daughter or her new husband. When he was quiet, he slinked back down the cave until he reached his daughter's nest. He needed to talk to her dragon mate, Crown Prince Alex, and tell her what he had done.

———

Just down the hallway, Nick slipped into his own nest. He was a sunrise dragon, but just three months ago, had married his love, Sadie Diya. Sadie was a summer dragon, and her father was King of Terrek.

Their marriage had been fraught with controversy. Never had shifter dragons from different clans taken each other as formal mates. Their wedding had been a disaster. Forced to have a joint wedding with his older brother, the two brides had fought tooth and nail through every detail.

The ceremony had done nothing but make Nick and Sadie even more bitter. Forced to share their special day, they felt they had been upstaged by his older brother. And it didn't help that the sorcerer was obviously in on it. He had done some kind of mumbo jumbo with his staff, causing blue light to flow over his brother and his bride, and declaring them blessed by the Dragon God.

No such light had been delivered over Sadie and Nick, and it had been humiliating. Combined with what Nick could only assume was an unfortunately timed earthquake, and some shenanigans in which a disembodied voice from the crowd had declared themselves the Dragon God and had shouted into the crowd, "I withhold my blessing. I am angry. I am coming!" they had been left in disgrace.

Honestly, if it was in his power, he would throw that sassy sorcerer, Darius Fletcher, into the dungeon. But he did not hold the keys, and it wasn't in his power. Soon, though, he could take revenge on all who stood in his way or wronged him, and he would take the throne of Dumara.

These past three months, he had been plotting and planning, growing his base of dragon malcontents. Later, he would change into his human form, and go hang out in the Rusty Shield, the preferred hangout of the soldiers of Dumara when they were off duty. He had been building his base of human malcontents as well. He would need every person and dragon possible to pull off his coup. It was all coming together.

He entered his cave. It had been the Chuvash family cave before his mother's sudden death. It contained three rings of boulders. The large middle nest had been his parents', the one on the left his brothers'. Right before the wedding, his brother and Dahlia had moved down the hall, and their father had not occupied his nest much since Queen Cassandra's death, preferring to stay in his human form most of the time.

The assassination attempt that Nick had so carefully planned with their enemies to the north had gone wrong. His mother, instead of his father, had flown out to meet the sun that morning and had been attacked. She had died of her wounds, and his father had been grief stricken ever since.

Nick had not meant for his mother to die, but she was a necessary loss. He missed her, and she had been the one to always smooth things over between his older brother and him. She had made excuses for her youngest son, calling him moody. In reality, she had been the only one who really cared for him, and now she was gone.

He had his Sadie though, and she was resting in their nest, to the far right. Her dark green scales looked almost black in the gloom of the caves. She opened her orange eyes, and they were full of love. "My mate. Come, keep us warm," she demanded, scooting over to make room for him.

He smiled. In the middle of their nest was the egg of their dragonling. Normally, dragon eggs were the colors of the sun, red, orange, yellow, gold, or on rare occasions, a pink color. Their egg was a dull bronze color. Nick assumed it was because their son would be a hybrid, a mix of summer and sunrise. Light and fire. He couldn't wait to meet his dragonling. The egg would hatch soon, just a few more weeks.

He carefully lowered his hulk into his nest, settling carefully around the egg and Sadie. He licked her neck, and she settled her head on his flank, content.

Nick grimaced a little when she inadvertently touched his burned spot. He would have to have his Dragon Keeper put some balm on it later, before he shifted into his human form to go upstairs.

"Oh, what happened? You've been singed!" Sadie exclaimed, looking at the scales on his hindquarters, which were charred and curled up on the edges.

"Torrid wanted to have a little talk with me. Things got heated," Nick said, not wanting to tell his mate that Torrid had dominated him, and he had run away.

"Dahlia's father. I hate that family," Sadie said, spitting and looking cross. "Love, you probably haven't heard. Dahlia laid a dragonling egg today."

"Not surprising. That has been my brother's goal to come up with an heir as quickly as possible. The two have certainly been working hard at it." Nick smirked.

Sadie looked smug. "Our son will be older by three months."

Nick growled, "Not that it matters. But soon, my father and brother will be out of the way. The first thing I will do after my brother's last breath is to smash that egg, and then I think I'll give

Dahlia to Quartz. He needs a mate, and no other female will take him."

Sadie chuckled. "I would love to see Dahlia forced to take Quartz as a mate, but he's so small and feeble, I think she would crush him. She's a big drakaina, after all."

"You could take her, love. Well, you might need to cheat a little, but all's fair in love and war."

"It certainly is." She blinked her eyes adoringly and settled in for a rest.

———

Alex Chuvash, the Crown Prince of Dumara, couldn't be prouder. It wasn't a surprise that Dahlia had produced an egg, as they had known for a few weeks now that a dragonling was on its way, but the placement of the egg in the nest was a big occasion in the clan. People had been coming by all day to give their congratulations.

The egg was golden yellow and streaked with red, and Dahlia told him it was a male dragon. Already, the egg was larger than normal, a good sign.

He was delighted when the Dragon Keepers, Mila and Aswin, had come in earlier. They looked over the egg, tapping it a few times, and declaring it fit and fine. "Congratulations," Mila said with excitement, genuinely happy for the pair. Technically, Mila was HIS Dragon Keeper, bound to him. They shared a telepathic link that allowed them to speak across distance and share thoughts. They were very close, and early on, love had blossomed between the two.

Since his wedding, she had distanced herself, mostly to protect her heart, but also out of respect. She adored Dahlia and wouldn't do anything to jeopardize her position as Dragon Keeper. She loved her job and tended to her charges every day with a smile and tenderness.

Her father, Aswin Fletcher, had been the Dragon Keeper since before she was born. He was bound to King Rand and shared the telepathic link with him. When King Rand died, he would retire, and Mila would become the full-time Keeper.

"Very good, Dahlia. King Rand is thrilled. He will come down in a bit, to give his congratulations," Aswin said, running his hand over the gold and red egg, shining in the dim light of the cave.

"I wish my mother could be here to meet her grand dragonling," Dahlia said sadly. Her mother had died two weeks after her wedding of a wasting disease. She had lasted longer than most had thought, but when she died, she was just a shell of her former self. They had interred her with great sadness and fanfare in the dragon catacombs, deep within the mountain, next to the bones of her ancestors.

Just then, Torrid came in, looking perturbed. "Ahh, the Dragon Keepers. You may need to pay a visit to Nick. We had a little meeting in the hall, and I lost my temper. He may be slightly singed."

"Torrid," Aswin said disapprovingly, shaking his head.

Aswin felt King Rand in his thoughts. The name Torrid had caught his attention. "What has Torrid done, Aswin?" Rand thought to his Dragon Keeper from his study in the castle. He had court today and was just putting his notes away after a meeting with the diplomat from Norda.

"It appears Nick and Torrid had a heated discussion about his little group of friends. Nick continues to sow discord in the caves, and Torrid called him out on it," Aswin said, after listening to the explanation given by the fierce warrior.

"I should really spend more time in the caves. I'll come down tonight," Rand thought, closing up his notes. He stood and took off his crown and his ermine robe and glanced quickly at the decorated mirror that stood just outside the attached bathroom.

He was an older man, nearing fifty. He had brown, graying hair, with a short beard. His striking blue eyes looked wise, and he thought he didn't look bad for a man his age. He shifted and flew every morning with his clan, and it had kept him in very good shape. He was muscular and lean, even though he was no longer a young dragon.

What he really needed to do was to talk to Nick. The boy needed a diversion. He had entirely too much time on his hands, and he wasn't using his time in any positive way. Rand kept Alex busy, helping him with official functions, but Nick was pretty much left to his own devices.

He looked back over his correspondence from Norda, the human kingdom that covered the entire southern continent. They were a fierce seafaring race, and they had the biggest navy in the world. They had been begging him to meet with them. It appeared pirates were plaguing the trading routes to the south. He knew they wanted firm agreements as to safe passage to Dumara and all lands east and west.

He had been building a small fleet of ships to fight the privateers and protect Sunrise Bay, but he didn't know if he wanted to reveal his plans yet to Norda. He could send Nick to Norda, as a diplomat. It would get him out of the way for the time being and allow Alex to firm up his support in his absence.

It was perfect. He just needed to convince Nick of it, which would be his biggest challenge. With a sigh, he put down his notes and headed downstairs. Maybe he would sleep in his nest tonight.

CHAPTER 2

THE SORCERER OF DUMARA

Three months ago, on the fateful day that both Princes had married in a joint ceremony, Darius Fletcher, Sorcerer of Dumara, had hightailed it out of that cathedral so fast he left people's heads spinning.

Aware he had just been a part of the most scandalous wedding in hundreds of years and had invoked the wrath of his boss, the Dragon God, he had been hiding out for the past three months. He really hoped that everyone would forget his involvement sooner rather than later, especially King Rand and his festering blight of a son, Nick Chuvash.

For the last three months, he had been hearing two distinct death drumbeats. He thought about brewing up another batch of noctum, a powerful potion that bestowed visions or caused instant death, but thought he might be pushing his luck. It was apparent things had been set in motion. He was in his workshop, with his staff firmly clamped in a vice on his bench. He was trying to scry into the veta stone sat on the top, but the murky depths of the jewel refused to give up its secrets.

All the sudden, his early warning spell went off, and he cursed.

It had been a quiet few months, and he did not want guests today, or any day really.

He glanced out the door and quickly changed his mind. It was Gayle, the Dragon Keeper of Fresthav. The pair has spent a memorable night together, about six months ago.

In a panic, he ran to his bathroom, washed his face, brushed his hair, and even threw on a clean robe. Luckily, he had taken a bath just a few days ago, so he didn't even smell rank.

Acting nonchalant, he walked to his door and threw it open just as she came up the walk. Linnea Stellen, Crown Princess of Fresthav, was sitting in his front yard. She was a sky-blue dragon with a white tail. She looked bored, and sat down, tucking her wings close to her body, and then spreading out in the snow. Soon, it would be spring, and the ice dragons would retreat to their kingdom, where it was cooler all year long.

"Gayle, a pleasure," he said, giving her a little bow.

"Oh, Darius. How are you today?" she said, giving him a quick grin and a peck on the cheek. His heart started hammering, and he felt a flush creep to his cheeks.

Gayle was wearing a pair of tight-fitting black riding pants. She threw off her white furs, revealing a form-fitting white sweater.

"I'm uhhh, good," he said, stammering. "Please come in. Have some tea, stay a while."

She smiled and accepted his invitation, moving into his space with grace. As she brushed by him, he caught the sweet scent of astra flowers, and it hit him square in the gut.

He put the kettle on the woodstove and set out two mugs. Soon, they were sipping them, and Gayle was looking at him intently.

"I need a little something stronger than tea. I hope you don't mind." She pulled a flask out of her boot, and then with a shrug opened it and gulped it down, nearly in one pull.

Darius's eyes nearly popped out of his head. "What is that?" he asked. He had never seen a woman drink like that.

"Iseiki. Give me about fifteen minutes for this to take effect, and then I'll tell you what I came here for."

"Well, if you're drinking at 2 o'clock in the afternoon, maybe I'll have a drink as well," he said, getting up, and grabbing his jug of Blythe's Best from his workbench. He poured a little into his tea and took a sip with a grin.

"I don't know how you drink that stuff." Gayle laughed. It was a belly laugh, and it sounded like it came from her soul. Darius thought she looked impossibly beautiful. She was, in fact, the only girl he had been attracted to since Leah. His first doomed love.

"I really don't. I'm just trying to keep up with you, and obviously failing miserably."

"I have a reason for getting ugly drunk so early in the day, but you'll have to wait a minute. Tell me, while we are waiting, about these drumbeats I've been hearing. Everyone just brushes them off, but they feel wrong somehow."

"So you hear them too?" Darius said, shocked. He thought he was the only one.

"I have heard them every day for about three months. Princess Linnea and Queen Thora hear them, although no one else seems to. That is one reason I came today. They sound ominous and make my skin crawl," she said, feeling the effects of the alcohol. She was warm, and she unbuttoned the first few buttons of her sweater. Her face was flushed, and she could feel her mind connection with Thora Stellen, Queen of Fresthav, slipping away. Just a few more minutes, and she could talk to Darius without worrying that the Queen would eavesdrop.

"I know what they are, and I'm afraid I've played a bigger part in this than I care to admit." He got up, searching through his pile of papers for his tome of the Dragon God. He found the old crumbling document and pulled it out. He found the bookmark where he had left it, when he started searching through the tome desperately, right after the wedding debacle. He opened it to the bookmark and began reading.

The Book of the Dragon God - The Final Judgment

11 The end shall be foretold, with the reputation by the snake. The first beat will drum, and that shall be a warning of the things to come.

12 And four shall wed, but only two shall receive the blessing. Earthquakes will spell thy doom, and the drums shall beat. This is a sign to turn from the path.

13 A king shall fall, and the snake will rise, killing the innocent and beginning his reign of terror. The third beat will join the chorus, and the Dragon King will turn his full attention to the world. Droughts, famine, and war shall sweep the land, and all hope will be lost.

14 The fourth beat signals all to gather at the rock from which Mo departed. The Dragon God will descend, and darkness will fall. He will judge those dragons who remain and find them either worthy or lacking. The worthy will be rewarded, and the unworthy will be destroyed.

15 The fifth beat will fall, and one by one all will fade away, leaving only the bones of the earth, and the animals and the humans will be the only ones who remain. All dragons will disappear, and the Dragon God will be no more on this fair earth.

"I've never read that part," Gayle admitted. "In fact, I haven't read much of the Book of the Dragon God. I guess I should have. It seems all like scary stuff." Her words slurred, and her eyes became unfocused. Thora was so far away now, just a faint whisper in her mind.

"I've got to admit, I'm scared. I didn't really put this together until the wedding of Sadie and Nick, and the earthquake started. My staff started smoking, and a disembodied voice spoke, refusing to bless their marriage. I started hearing the drumbeats soon after that."

"I see. And the next step is the death of a king. It could be any one of them, really. Everyone but Queen Thora."

"Yes. And I'm worried. Everything seems quiet now, but who knows what evil plots lurk in the background."

They sat in silence for a moment, thinking of which king might die. It was hopeless. They simply didn't have enough information.

"Well, this is all fascinating. I promise I'll read more into this when I get home. If I think of anything, I'll send you the news. But since the spirits have kicked in, I'm ready to tell you why I really came here," Gayle said. She was really drunk now and knew if she tried to walk, she would probably fall down.

All of a sudden, Darius knew why she had drunk so much, so quickly. "You're trying to sever the connection, aren't you?" he said, looking at her with wide eyes.

"Yep! I discovered this quite by accident after one-too-many glasses of wine one night. Bloody useful, Queen Thora is always watching," Gayle said, giggling, thinking of the Queen's distaste in her choice of men.

Darius was a little disappointed. "I guess you didn't fly here just to see me then. What do you want to talk to me about?"

"It's Thora. Both Linnea and I are worried about her. She's been acting more irrational than normal. Last week, she killed one of her top advisors for suggesting that perhaps we should expand trade with Dumara. Anything that remotely contradicts her, and she flies off into a rage. I'm honestly afraid for my life. I dare not speak anything against the Queen. Linnea toes the line, but even she is worried. The Queen is paranoid of everyone and everything, and takes to wandering the dragon halls at night in her human form, speaking gibberish and making wild claims."

"Thora is rather old, isn't she? She was an old woman when I became a sorcerer, and that's been thirty years."

"She is. She turned 105 this year. Linnea and I think it's time for her to step down and give the throne to Linnea, especially now since Linnea has her own heir. But of course, no one dares suggest this to Thora."

"Hmmm. And you came here for my advice or help?" Darius asked, looking at her with his soft brown eyes.

"Both really. We don't know what to do. Is there any potion or spell that could help her? Even if it's just bringing her to her senses again."

"We can try to give her the potion of youth. I don't think she's ever asked for it. It will turn back the clock a little bit. But she's so old, the side effects will be severe. The older you get, the longer it takes to work. At 105, she may sleep for a month after she takes it.

She'll wake up feeling much younger and refreshed, but I don't know how much it will help her state of mind. It's really just for the body, not the soul." Darius got up and began rummaging around his workbench. "Ahh, I knew I had some left. I made up a batch a while back for Doyle, Dragon Keeper of Murdad. He's only 85, but he needs it now a few times a year to keep spry."

"I didn't bring any gold, but I've got to admit that was sort of on purpose. I had another reason to come today, and it involved you," Gayle said with a laugh. She got up and looked at him seductively.

"Oh," was all Darius said, and a grin spread across his face. "I've got to admit, I was kind of hoping you would show back up again. I thought about sending flowers and chocolates after the last visit, but the distance is a bit far, and I don't have the luxury of traveling by dragon."

"I get lonely, all by my lonesome in Fresthav. Being a Dragon Keeper is a tough job, and all of the men in the castle are afraid of me," she said, pulling a dagger out of her boot and laying it on the table. She started unbuttoning her shirt, stumbling a little as she moved to him.

"I wouldn't begin to know why," he chuckled, and then she was on him, like a wild woman, kissing him and biting his neck. He ran his fingers through her long black hair and looked at her full of longing.

"I like you, Darius. I hope you like me too," she said, her full lips close to his ear. Shivers went down his spine, and he drifted his hands over her, closing his eyes against the intensity of his feelings.

"You're bad news, Gayle. But then again, so am I," Darius chuckled, and then led her upstairs to his bed, shooing his cat off it before pulling her down and giving her his full attention.

CHAPTER 3

KILLING FIELDS

I t had been a while since Alex had gone hunting with the clan. He had been so preoccupied with his own life that he had been neglecting chores such as this. But now that Dahlia and he had created a new life, he felt a little of the pressure receding.

Torrid had come by his nest this morning on his way out and asked his son-in-law if he wanted to go with the hunting party this morning. Dahlia had nudged him out of the nest. "Go! You are driving me crazy, love. We will be fine."

So here he was, wings spread, with the brown fields of winter below him. It has been a snowy season, but spring was around the corner. Warmer days had melted the blanket of white, leaving the skeletal branches of trees reaching for the sky from the ground.

The brown fields made it harder to see the deer that they hunted, so they turned north to the Great Divide. The forests surrounding the southern foothills were thick with deer, and the lack of leaves on the trees now was an advantage.

He was flying today with Torrid, Tyre, Apple, and Chain. They were in formation, their eyes flicking between the ground and the horizon. This far north, there was a good chance they would run into nightfall dragons, but all the better. Alex was feeling up for a little skirmish this morning.

Below, a family of deer leapt a stream and caught his attention. A mother, father, and baby. He wouldn't take the mother, leaving her to raise the baby, but the father was fair game.

He dropped, claws outstretched, and struck the stag with a slashing blow. Before it even knew what had hit it, it was dead on the ground, its life blood spilled around it. The female paused, looking at him in fear, but knowing what was good for it, took off with lightning speed, the doe following closely behind. The pair would find some nice bit of scrub brush and hide.

He circled around and then picked up his catch. He had already eaten this morning, but this would make a tasty morsel for Dahlia.

Apple and Chain were working together to his left. They had spotted a larger group. Chain was driving them east, straight into Apple's claws. With a roar, Apple grabbed two stags, one in each claw.

Chain took the advantage of the terrified stags and grabbed two of his own. It had been a very successful morning. Chain and Apple circled around them, and finally they were back in formation.

"What do you say, head back now, or let Torrid grab a few?" Chain asked. He was a golden dragon, but he had unusual coloring for a sunrise dragon. He had silver scales, somewhat randomly, throughout his body. The Dragon Keeper Aswin had said it was just a rare genetic mutation, as no other sunrise dragon had any silver in their coloring at all. They were all some combination of gold, red, or orange.

Alex turned his golden head, his mane ruffling in the breeze. "Let's get back. We've been lucky today not to run into any nightfall dragons."

Apple was beating his red wings next to him. "I agree. Let's go back." They turned to the west, and now they had a headwind.

It was not twenty minutes later when their luck ran out. Torrid was flying point when he spotted them. "Nightfall dragons to the north, looks like four of them!"

Immediately, they all threw down their deer carcasses into the field below. They could collect them later after they ran these interlopers out of their territory.

Murdad, the kingdom to the north, was a dead land. While some animals did roam, they were harder to come by. The nightfall dragons loved to hunt in their hunting grounds, where pickings were easy and they could skirmish with their enemies the sunrise dragons.

The four dark purple dragons were headed directly for them, their yellow eyes full of malice and their dark wings beating the air quickly.

The two groups of dragons collided in a clash of teeth and claws. Roars rent the air as they made another pass.

Alex rolled to his right, narrowly missing a blast of dark magic. He retaliated with his own roar, and burst of light magic, hitting one attacker full in the face.

The purple dragon shrieked with pain and turned his full attention to Alex, diving fast. Alex didn't have time to change course, and he felt the nightfall dragon's teeth rip into his front leg. Searing pain hit him as the poison from the dragon's teeth poured into his bloodstream.

Now Alex was angry. He twisted and hit the nightfall dragon with his hind legs, his claws slashing across the dragon's already burned face. The dragon shrieked again and gave up. He turned to the north to retreat, calling for his brothers to join him.

One by one, the nightfall dragons disengaged. Until there was only one, fiercely battling Tyre.

Tyre was a maroon dragon, with a dark yellow underbelly. A little on the smaller side, he made up for his small size with the largest set of fangs and horns Alex had ever seen. He had suffered a wing injury, and part of his wing flapped in the wind.

As the last nightfall dragon came in for another strike, Tyre lowered his head. His horns, spirals above his forehead, slashed into the side of the dragon. A rain of blood fell as the enemy screamed in pain, turning and diving as quickly as possible.

Soon, all the nightfall dragons had retreated out of sight, and they flew back to where they had dropped their deer, slowly nursing their injuries. They landed to take stock.

Alex's leg was badly gashed, but he would be fine. Tyre's wing injury was a concern. By flying on it, he could make it worse.

Chain had been slightly singed, but nothing too serious.

"Rest a moment and let me think," Alex said to the dragons. They complied, settling down.

Mila had been in the background of his thoughts. They shared a mental connection and could speak through their minds across vast distances. "Mila, we have a few injuries," he thought to her, and then detailed what those injuries were.

"That wing tip doesn't look that bad," she thought to him. "He should be able to make it back home if the wind isn't that strong, and you take it easy. Your leg looks nasty. Dad and I will meet you at the caves."

"Thanks, Mila," he said, and pushed back the connection. They were both much better now at this, and it was easier now to allow each other to fade into the background. Unlike when they had first been connected by her uncle the sorcerer, and every thought and action had come through.

"Be more careful next time!" she said, sternly, from the back of his thoughts.

He chuckled, and then turned to his squad. "We are going to head back, but slowly. We don't want that wing tear to get any worse."

They picked up their deer and rose out of the sky. A farmer, who had been watching from a fair distance, looked in awe as the pack of brilliantly colored dragons rose into the air. Spotting a sunrise dragon was thought to be good luck, and he just had five of them land in his field.

———

Alex threw his deer on the kill pile, which had now grown tall from all the morning hunting. His Dragon Keeper, Mila, was standing with her arms crossed, glaring at him.

"Alex," she demanded, "let me see that injury!"

"Cut him some slack, Mila," her father, Aswin Fletcher, pleaded. He was looking over Tyre's wing injury. "Yeah, this is easily fixed. Head to your nest, and I'll be there shortly." He patted Tyre's rump as he moved off.

Aswin moved over to Alex, looking at his front leg. He bent down, his brown eyes scrutinizing the cut. "Looks like it hurts like hell. I can see the purple poison from here. You're going to have to wash this out good, Mila. There is a bottle of Blythe's Best tucked in that chest by the first intersection. Grab that on your way by."

A nasty laugh echoed from the nearby hallway. Nick appeared out of the shadows, his red scales catching the light. "Did my brother get a boo boo while he was out pretending to be a leader?"

"Shut it, Nick. When was the last time you went out hunting, huh?" The growl came out almost unbidden.

"Well, it's been a while. You know, we are waiting on pins and needles for my son to be born. I heard Dahlia set an egg. It would be a shame if something happened to it." Nick's dragon mouth sneered as he glared at his older brother.

Aswin flicked a glance to Nick and his voice was deadly. "Something better not happen to it Nick. I'm warning you."

"Hoo ho! The Dragon Keeper is taking a side. Not unexpected. Don't worry, I wouldn't touch that egg. I've got better things to do." Nick slinked back down the hallway, chuckling to himself. He wouldn't lay a claw on that egg, but one of his minions would be happy to, if only given the chance.

"Head back to your nest," Mila said to Alex, but looking after Nick with concern. "I'll be there shortly."

———

Alex limped back down the hallway, his huge dragon body screaming in pain as the poison coursed through him. While the poison wouldn't kill him, it was meant to incapacitate an enemy, leaving them distracted from the pain. If left untreated, he would be in so much pain he wouldn't be able to move.

He passed his brother's nest and heard the sounds of his brother's low rumbles from within. Sadie's high-pitched giggle rang in his ears, and he knew that his loathsome little brother was probably mocking him. Well, whatever. Nick wasn't worth the attention. The two brothers had been rivals since the day Nick had been born, and occasionally, they had been known to come to blows.

Just a few caves down was his and Dahlia's nest, and he had to admit, he had been happy she had wanted to move to their own cave. At first, they had shared the large Chuvash family cave with their father, brother and Sadie, as was custom in the dragon clan.

Since his mother's death, their father Rand rarely slept in his nest, leaving the two brothers to share the space.

Ironically, it had been Dahlia who had suggested the move. Nick's choice of mate, a summer dragon named Sadie from the neighboring Kingdom of Terrek had made cohabitation with his brother impossible.

They had been friends with King Dayia and his family for their entire lives. But he would have never guessed that Sadie Dayia, the spoiled Princess of Terrek, would become his sister-in-law.

First of all, she was a summer dragon, and never in the history of the four dragon clans had two dragons from different clans taken each other as bound mates. Sure, there had been dalliances before, and hybrids had been born, but they were usually exiled from their clans, forced to live on the edges of society, alone.

Now, Sadie had laid the bronze egg, and a Prince of Dumara would be born with both light and fire. Nick took great pleasure in rubbing it all in their faces that his son would have dual powers.

He entered his cave, and Dahlia immediately saw him limping. "Alex! What happened? Are you okay?" Dahlia's red and yellow body was wrapped around their egg, her yellow eyes filled with concern.

"I'll be fine," he said, grimacing, settling down on his haunches. "A little hunting accident."

"That's no accident. You got into a skirmish," she challenged him.

"Yes, we did. We had a successful hunt and encountered some nightfall dragons on the way home."

"I worry about you so, Alex."

Just then, Mila appeared, carrying her bag. "Don't worry, Dahlia. This isn't that bad. The treatment is probably going to be worse than the injury." Alex tried to ignore her scent as she put her bag between his legs. She smelled of the astra perfume she always wore, which drove him crazy. She tucked a strand of her brown curly hair behind her ear as she peered inside the bag.

He loved this woman deeply, and they had shared one night of passion before he had married Dahlia. What he wouldn't give to be with her forever, but he had his duty.

She caught his thought and looked up at him with a smile. She was thinking the same thing, but she pushed the thought away. After clearing her throat, she held up the jug. "This is going to hurt, my friend. Sorry."

"Let's get it over with," he grumbled.

She climbed on his ankle, straddling it between her legs. The bite mark was a little farther up his leg, a crescent of pain. She looked at him, pursed her lips, and started pouring the spirits on his leg.

He howled in pain as the cheap alcohol poured into the rent, washing out the poison. He tilted his head to the ceiling, and a light beam hit the stone ceiling above him. In his agony, he had pulled back his front leg, and Mila went flying.

"Sorry," he gasped, holding out his leg again.

"No problem," she said with a smile. "I managed to not even break the bottle. One more time, and then I'll bandage this with some healing balm. I don't think you need stitches for this one."

"Okay, get it over with," he grimaced, preparing for the sting of the liquor. It came, but he tensed up, and avoided throwing off Mila again. He wanted to cry from the pain, but he kept the tears from falling.

Mila took out a tin of healing balm, rubbing the thick greasy paste over his wound. The balm felt soothing and smelled like honey. "That's better," he said, closing his eyes.

She took out a roll of bandages and wrapped his leg tight. "You heal fast. By tomorrow, it will be right as rain." Climbing back down from his leg, she packed up her bag.

"Thank you, Dragon Keeper," Dahlia said. "I'll make sure he rests. You know how he gets. Always pacing."

"I've got a lot on my mind!" he defended himself as he slipped into his nest next to Dahlia and their egg.

Mila looked at him kindly. "I know, Alex. Don't greet the sun tomorrow, and rest. We will be back tomorrow to check on you. Be well," she thought to him. If Dahlia hadn't been nearby, she might have given him a tender kiss on his dragon head, but she didn't. Instead, she turned and headed out of the hallway to join her father in sewing up Tyre's torn wing.

———

Later, Mila and her father took the path down from the caves. Both of them walked slowly. It had been a long day. The sun was just setting to the west, and it was a beautiful sunset.

The sky was red and golden, with the last rays of the sun catching the clouds above. A warm breeze was in the air, promising spring. "It'll be the change of seasons soon. I wonder if Sadie is going to fly to greet it with her brethren."

"Will they still accept her? Her parents didn't even come to the wedding, and as far as I know, there has been no communication between them for months."

"I don't know. That's a good question. King Cleon Dayia has been quiet for months. I know the summer dragons have been patrolling the north, as per the alliance agreement, but we've only heard from their diplomats," Aswin pondered. "Well, I guess we will find out shortly."

Mila nodded as her feet slipped on the steep path. Her father grabbed her arm. "Careful, Mila," he ordered, and then grinned. "One of these days, I will not be here to catch you when you stumble."

"Oh, Father! Don't say that!" She looked at him sadly. She couldn't imagine doing this job without her father at her side. He was a strong, silent force, lending her his vast knowledge when needed.

He reached the end of the trail, and the stepping stones that lead across the river. "Well, I'm not getting any younger, Mila," he said with a laugh, and then hopped across the stones easily.

Mila followed, and the two of them stepped onto the road that led into the town of Dumara. Main Street was busy tonight, and the streets were filled with townspeople enjoying the warmer weather.

Restaurants were full of chatting people and the smells of rich dinner, and the quaint shops that lined the street were just closing for the night.

The mercantile that was right next door to their shop was just closing, and old Finn gave them a toothless grin and a wave.

Their shop was on the corner. The sign above the door read "Dragon Keeper of Dumara, Aswin Fletcher." The sign on the green door read "OPEN." The store was lit inside, and Mila could see their shopkeeper, Sam Arbuckle, moving around.

Mila threw open the door, changing the sign to "CLOSED."

"Hello, good evening, you two. Have a good day up at the caves?" Sam asked, as he paused to count the till. He blushed, and Mila couldn't help but wonder if he still didn't have a crush on her. It had been a problem in the past, but she had hoped that with his marriage, he had gotten over his previous infatuation.

"Busy today," Aswin said. "A group of dragons got caught in a bit of skirmish. A few minor injuries to take care of."

"I'm going to need some more healing balm," Mila said, setting her bag down on the counter. Inside was everything she needed to take care of dragons, all the potions, balms, and even herbs to make potions on the fly. It was her most cherished possession, and she rarely let it out of her sight. Her father had the same bag, and he had them specially made by the leather maker in town. They were incredibly sturdy and were mostly waterproof.

Sam turned and grabbed a tin of balm off the shelf and then stuck it quickly in her bag. "Anything else?"

"Could you go next door tomorrow and buy two more gallons of Blythe's Best? We are out in the caves."

"Sure, no problem," Sam said, making a note.

"Can you tell Kiera that I want to see her soon? Can I stop by Sunday for a chat?" Mila asked. Sam and Kiera had been married just a few months before, and they lived across the street with her parents in their tailor shop. During the day, she worked for her parents, and he worked here. It wasn't optimal, but they were saving up money to buy a house, in the hopes they could start a family soon.

"I will do so. I know she's been wanting to have a good visit with you. The shop has been quiet lately, and her parents are out of town, on a buying trip to Tiago. She's been closing up the shop and meeting me over here to have lunch together. That is one good thing about living across the street with my in-laws," he chuckled.

"Sam, why don't we give Mila the day off? You can come up to the caves with me tomorrow, and we will close the shop. We haven't closed in a while. We can check on the injured, and then we can gather some astra flowers in the afternoon."

"Sounds good, boss," Sam said with a grin. He loved going to the caves with them, something he rarely got to do. He loved dragons just as much as they did, but the store was his main focus.

"A day off! How luxurious. Normally, my boss is a taskmaster." Mila took off her jacket and hung it on a hook near the door. "Well, I'm headed upstairs. I think I'll heat up that stew left over from yesterday."

"I've got a few things I want to do in the workshop. I need to take inventory. We need astra flowers, and we are probably out of other things as well." Aswin scanned the shelves behind them. They were full, which meant that Sam had been making potions.

Mila ran upstairs to their cozy little apartment. The fire in the woodstove needed starting, and she shoved in a few logs and some kindling, starting it with one of the long matches they kept in the cupboard. Soon, the woodstove was ready. She opened their icebox and found the leftovers from yesterday still in the pot. She plopped the pan on the stove, happy she wouldn't have to cook tonight.

Soon, it was warmed, and she scooped out a bowl for herself. There was enough for her father also, so she pushed the pan off the hottest part of the stovetop.

She sat down at the table and dug in. She didn't realize how hungry she was until she started eating. As was the norm, they had missed lunch, not bothering to come down from the caves.

She reached out to Alex with her mind connection. "How are you doing?"

"I'm good, Mila. Don't worry about me, please. I've got enough to handle with Dahlia. She's been extra anxious lately, with the egg and all."

"It's my job to care about you, Alex. I'll worry if I please," she said, letting him feel her sass.

"Oh, Mila. Never change," he chuckled. "I'm going to sleep. Goodnight, my love."

That surprised Mila. He had never called her love before. She felt warm inside, glad to know he still cared about her.

After dinner, she curled up on her couch with one of her favorite books, Beowulf, an epic story about a king who goes on an adventure to slay a dragon. It was, of course, written by a human and from his point of view. Mila always felt bad for the dragon, who was just trying to live his life peacefully until someone tried to steal his treasure. She was always secretly pleased when Beowulf died.

Her black cat, Jinx, meowed at her, and she petted him while he sat on her lap.

It was a while before Aswin appeared, ladling out his own bowl of stew.

"King Rand is concerned about Nick. He's going to send him away," Aswin said after Mila put her book down. That was one thing she loved about her father. He never bothered her when she had her nose in a book.

"Really? Where to?" Mila asked, curious.

"Norda. He has plans to put all that scheming to work. He wants to make Nick a diplomat." Aswin blew on his stew. It had gotten boiling hot sitting on the back of the stove.

"Will one of us have to go with him?" Mila asked, concerned. She did not want to have to fly across the sea to Norda on the back of Nick. She had never ridden him, and she didn't quite trust him to deliver her safely.

"No. He'll have to take a boat. He won't have a Dragon Keeper, so he's going to have to stay in human form. Besides, the Norda don't take well to dragons. They hate them and prohibit any in their lands. You know the history."

"Yes," Mila said, thinking of the Book of the Dragon God, on the shelf just to the right of her. It told the story of the coming of the Dragon God, and the people who were here before he arrived. The humans had rebelled against him and the four dragon kings and had tried to escape by boat. After many trials and tribulations, they had arrived at the southern continent and set up their own kingdom, away from the reach of the dragons.

"My brother will not like that plan," Alex said in her mind. He apparently was still awake.

"I thought you were going to sleep?" Mila asked, deciding she would head to bed now. She closed her book and gave Jinx one last pet before getting up.

"I know, I nearly was, but I caught that thought. My Father is right to find something for Nick to do, but he hates being in human form. He will not want to leave Sadie and his dragonling, to go play diplomat in Norda. It's just not going to happen."

CHAPTER 4

A VISIT

Mila had a terrible dream that night. She tossed and turned, her sheets wrapped around her, tears running down her face in her sleep. She awoke with a start, gasping for air, her eyes flying open. Bolting upright, the visions of death and destruction of the city of Dumara were still vivid in her mind. She heard the two drumbeats, and then a voice seemed to speak to her out of the dark. "He will die, but will arise again. He is the chosen one."

Totally freaked out, Mila quickly lit her lamp on her bedside, and it threw a dim glow over her room. The door squeaked open, and her black cat Jinx stared at her with his green eyes. He jumped up on her bed and kneaded her, begging for pets. She laughed, and then patted him. She pulled the Book of the Dragon God off her nightstand where she had left it last night and started reading it again until her eyes grew heavy and her mind calmed. Then, with a sigh, she blew out her lamp and turned back over in her bed. Jinx settled in next to her, and for the rest of the night, she slept dreamlessly.

She slept in late the next morning, something she rarely got to do. With a groan, she sat up and felt out to Alex.

"Good morning, Mila," he said in her thoughts. "Your father is here, taking off my bandages. Still a little sore, but much better today."

"Good morning, Alex," she smiled as she thought her greetings to him. "Since you can't fly, what are your plans for the day?"

"Nothing much. I think I'll go upstairs today and talk to my father about this deal with Nick. Try to discourage him. I just don't think it's a great idea."

"Be careful, Alex. Try not to get into a shouting match with your brother. He'll just twist your words," Mila warned.

"Funny, Dahlia said the same thing. I'll try."

Mila nodded, more to herself. If she had to lose Alex to a dragon, she was glad it was Dahlia. Smart as a whip, kind, and outspoken, she was exactly what he needed.

She got up and took a leisurely bath, braiding her hair up today. She put on one of her trademark pantsuits. This one was a golden yellow, and the tone set off the brown in her hair perfectly. She looked in the mirror, and her eyes looked sad. Vestiges of her bad dream last night still swirled in her head, and she tried to shake her head to clear it.

Going into the kitchen, she found the kettle still warm, so she poured herself a quick tea and sliced off a hunk of bread. Spreading it with butter and jam, she ate her quick breakfast by herself, looking out the window at the busy street. So many people, just living their lives, trying to get by. Farmers with their wagons coming to the big city market, their wives and children shopping in city stores.

It was quiet downstairs. Normally, the bells on the door would tinkle with customers at this time of day, but her father and Sam had already left for the caves. She skipped down the stairs, excited to have the whole day to herself. She was startled to see a shadow at the door. There was a loud knock, and the handle jiggled.

"Who can this be? Can't they see the shop is closed?" Mila

thought angrily. She went to the door to tell them to go away, and was surprised to see the outline of Nick Chuvash. He banged on the door again, so forcefully the glass in the frame jiggled. If he wasn't careful, he was going to break something.

Angrily, she wretched open the door, looking at him with irritation in her eyes. "What, Nick? Can't you read? We are closed today!" she said, pointing to the sign.

"I can read just fine, Mila." He said her name like he was saying something dirty. Her name rolled off his tongue like poison.

She opened the connection with Alex. "Do you see who is at my doorstep this morning?"

"Interesting. I'll watch. I wonder what he wants?" Alex said. She caught a vision of him in human form, moving down the hall. He must be headed upstairs to talk to his father already.

"I need a potion. You sell potions. The last time I checked, you worked under the authority of my father. So technically, you work for me," Nick said with a sneer, pushing inside.

"What do you need? You could have just asked my father. He's up in the caves today, and he can deliver to you anything you want."

"Yes, I am aware. I wanted to see the shop, though. I'm interested in all aspects of dragon keeping. It's quite the store you have here. Workshop in the back, I assume?" He perused the shelves, pulling a few things off the shelf and leaving them on the counter.

"Yes. We make all the items in the back, and we have stores of supplies in the basement. We have an apartment upstairs."

"But you and your father are usually in the caves. That boy, Sam, runs the store when you are not here? He makes the potions for you?" Nick looked around coldly.

"Yes. He is our shopkeeper. He helps us sometimes. For example, I'm supposed to have the day off today," Mila said with a little fire in her voice.

"Too bad for you, then. I'll take this, and I need several energy potions, and three astragenica."

Mila sighed. "I'm going to have to make the energy potions. It's not something we keep on hand. As for the astragenica, what do you need that for?"

"Oh, Mila," he said, stepping forward. He touched her check, looking at her with disdain. "It's really none of your business. So do as I say, or you might regret it." He settled his hand on the base of her throat and gave it a bit of a squeeze.

Inside her head, she felt Alex's fury. "How dare he threaten you! Wait until I get my hands on that little snake."

A chill ran down her spine. Nick just looked at her, like a dragon would look at prey. Her mouth ran dry. She thought she saw murder flicker across his face, and she swallowed. "Of course. You'll have to give me a moment to make it. I have the astragenica in my bag."

He lifted his hand off her jugular. It had been pulsing rapidly. He had scared her, good. The more scared she was, the more she would be compliant when he took the crown. He needed the potions as part of his plan. He already had the noctom, hidden behind a book in his room. Soon, his plan would be put in motion, but he needed to fly to Fresthav and Murdad first. Sadie would act as his Dragon Keeper. He couldn't give himself astragenica, and he would need the energy potions to make the round trip to Fresthav, Murdad, and back to Dumara in one day.

She quickly went into the back room, grabbed her apron and tied it on. Nick followed her too closely, and then sat down on a stool, watching her intently.

Alex was angry in her head. "You're going to make this for him?"

"Yes. He scares me. Besides, I AM the Dragon Keeper, Alex," she thought to him, trying not to feel the prickle of Nick's eyes on her skin.

"I'll come down to the shop and confront him! He'll be sorry he touched you!"

"No, Alex. By the time you get down here from the castle, the potion will be done, and he will be gone. Plus, he'll wonder how you knew he was here. Let's just keep this secret between us," Mila thought, gathering ginseng, sage, pennywort, golden root, and peppermint. She pulled out the Bunsen burner and found the small copper bowl that fit on top.

"What's all that for?" Nick asked suspiciously.

"All these things go into the potion. I couldn't tell you what each one does, only that they are all necessary." Mila poured a measure out of each ingredient and dumped it into the bowl. Out of spite, she put in a full measure of peppermint. She hoped he choked on it. She found the mineral oil in a tin can under the bench, and added it as a slow drizzle, stirring it to incorporate all the ingredients. It didn't take long to come together, and she turned off the burner to let it cool. She stood back and looked at him, crossing her arms. "I don't suppose you are paying for all this?"

"Ha. Good one. No," Nick said, sneering at her.

With a sigh, Mila pulled out a piece of paper. She went out to the front and noted what he had on the counter. Two tins of dragon balm, a bottle of calm, and, of course, the three bottles of astragenica and the two bottles of energy potion. The total came to nearly 250 banknotes, almost a full week of Sam's wages. She wrote the list on the paper with the total and stuffed it into the drawer so they could account for the loss in their books. They had never charged the king for any potions, but this seemed to be a special case, and he had taken a few items straight from the shelves, which meant they were already accounted for. Her father kept pristine books and would be angry if anything came up short.

The energy potion was cooled now, and she pulled out three bottles and a funnel, getting every drop poured into the bottles. She handed over the bottles to Nick and glared at him. "You can leave now," she said, pointing to the door.

"What? You aren't even going to bag this for me? Tut tut, Dragon Keeper. What kind of service are you providing customers?"

Mila rolled her eyes and then went to the front. She took the time to wrap each bottle in tissue, and then placed them in one of their nice paper bags with handles that featured the store branding. "Thank you for visiting the Dragon Keeper's store. Remember, for you, we make house visits!" she said, in an overly saccharine surgery voice.

Nick took the bag with a smirk and then left. Mila was glad to see him leave. She turned back to the workshop, cleaning up the mess from her impromptu work, and then headed across the street. She desperately wanted to talk to her best friend, Kiera. It had been a while since the girls had caught up.

———

As expected, she found Kiera working in her father's tailor shop, organizing bolts of fabric. Her mother was in the back room, putting away new fabric they had just bought from the mills in Tiago.

Mila noticed her friend looked drawn and tired, with black circles under her eyes. Kiera had always been a hard worker, but Mila wondered if she had been working too hard.

"Kiera. It's so good to see you!" Mila exclaimed, giving her friend a warm hug.

"Oh, Mila. It's so good to see you!" Kiera returned her hug, and then started putting the few bolts she had pulled out back on the shelves. "MOM!" she yelled to the back, "Mila and I are going out!"

"Sure, dear. No problem. Enjoy your visit," Judith Wright said from the back, coming out with a few bolts of denim she wanted to add to the display. "Mila, dear. It's been ages. Good to see you!"

"You also, Mrs. Wright," Mila said, and Kiera pulled her away with a laugh, practically pushing her out the door.

The two girls walked down the boardwalk, enjoying the sights and sounds of the day. They neared the square, and a juggler on one end entertained the crowd, managing three hoops at once. On the other end, a puppet show entertained a small group of adults. It was a more bawdy show for the older crowd.

Mila and Kiera found a bench near the bakery, and Mila popped inside for some sweet rolls. Together, the girls enjoyed their snack, the warm rolls and sweet sugar providing a delightful treat.

"So, Kiera. How is married life?" Mila asked. Just three months ago, Sam and Kiera had married in a quiet ceremony in the small neighborhood chapel just down the street. Mila had been the maid of honor and had presented the bride with a bouquet of astra flowers. She had made a special trip into the dragon caves to gather the flowers that morning. It was a rare and expensive gift, and Kiera had dried the petals of her wedding bouquet and made a sachet, which she now kept tucked into her wardrobe. Now, the pleasant and uplifting scent filled her room every time she opened the door, reminding her of her best friend.

Kiera giggled like a schoolgirl. "Sam is so sweet. He doesn't even mind living with my parents. We almost have enough saved up again for a house. Hopefully, we can find something before the baby is born."

Mila stopped with her bun halfway to her mouth, and a smile erupted over her face. "What? You and Sam are going to have a little one? Oh, Kiera! I'm so excited for you!" she practically shrieked, hugging her friend close.

"Yes, and you are going to be an honorary auntie. Both Sam and I are the only children, so you get the job!"

Mila wiped her tears away, as they were flowing freely. "Thank you. I would be honored to be an auntie."

"Oh, Mila. I'm sorry. I didn't mean to make you cry," Kiera said.

"No, no. It's fine. It just occurred to me I'll probably never have children of my own. But that's okay, I'll just borrow yours," she laughed, wiping her face. She didn't know why this was hitting her so hard. She was the one who had sworn off men. Besides her little spontaneous night with Alex, she had never considered dating anyone else. And even since that time, she had thoroughly ignored every man she encountered. It appeared there was only one man,

33

well dragon, for her, and he was thoroughly taken, with his own dragonling on the way.

"You'll meet someone, someday. Just don't give up hope," Kiera said, patting her hand on her sleeve. "Someone out there is going to meet you and decide you're the one."

"I doubt that, Kiera. You've met me. I'm entirely too independent and sassy. But it's fine, really." Mila waved it away, and then took another bite of her roll. "So have you thought of names?"

"We really haven't. Sam isn't interested in naming any child after his father, so that's out. Love my parents, but I want something unique. We'll see."

"I've always been partial to flower names," Mila said, thinking of all the dragons she named with flower names. Rose, Tulip, Holly, and Dahlia.

"Hmmm. That's nice. I'll have to think about that," Kiera said, cocking her head, her blond hair falling over one eye.

They spent the rest of the afternoon walking through the merchant district. Kiera splurged and bought an elegant grandmother mantle clock, a handsome cherry color, and decorated with dragons chasing their tails. "It will be perfect for our new home, and I know Sam will love it. He just loves dragons."

Mila bought some chocolates, sharing with Kiera as they walked home. It was now late in the afternoon, and as they came around the corner to the street where both of their parents' shops were, Mila was shocked to see Alex standing there, looking at her with his blue piercing eyes.

"Oh," Kiera said, feeling the heat flow between the two and looking back and forth between them. "I think I see Sam is back inside. I'm going to go show him the clock!"

"Hi, Mila," Alex said fiercely. He had a bowler hat on and a simple trench coat against the cold. His long blond hair was tied back, and he looked like any other merchant out for a stroll. "Walk with me?"

"Sure, Alex. I'm surprised to see you here. Want a chocolate?" she asked shyly, offering him one.

He looked at them, and then with a grin, picked one up and popped it in his mouth. A look of delight crossed his face. "That's good. I haven't had chocolate in ages."

"Mrs. Merry, the chocolatier in town, makes the best truffles. They are to die for."

"Well, I don't know about that, but they are pretty good," he admitted, offering her his arm. She took it, feeling his strong biceps under her hand. As always, he radiated heat. He probably didn't even need that coat to stay warm.

"What brings you to my side of town?" she asked, her voice dropping a little lower.

"I wanted to talk to you about my brother's visit. I let my father know what was going on, and he was just as shocked as I was. Neither of us has any idea why he would visit you to get potions. I didn't catch everything he wanted. What did he end up taking?"

"His order consisted of healing balm, a potion of calm, two energy potions, and three astragenicas. He didn't tell me what they were for, or how he was going to use them. He's going to need someone to give him the potions, obviously, but the entire visit was strange," Mila said, shivering, remembering his hand on her throat.

"He threatened you," Alex said, fire coming into his eyes. His fist clenched.

Mila nodded. "I was scared. I thought he might hurt me, and I was there all alone. It seemed best to do what he said."

"If he hurts you, I'll kill him." Alex nearly spat out the words, stopping in the street. He grabbed her by both arms. "You know I love you, Mila. I'm sorry. Dahlia and I . . . well, we have a dragonling coming. But there is no passion between us. We are just good friends. I can't even enjoy . . . ." He stopped; a slight hint of blush covered his face. He was going to tell her that making love to Dahlia was a chore. She complied, but it was obviously a chore for her also. Since the egg arrived, they had not touched each other once. He supposed his entire life would be a duty. And once he had a few children to secure his legacy, the rest of his life would be passionless and gray.

Mila touched his arm, and her lips brushed his cheek. She pulled him into the alley behind the store. It was narrow here, with just enough space for two people to stand side by side. He found her in his arms, his hands around her waist. She rested her head against his chest and sighed.

He moved his hands to her face and then found himself kissing her deeply and passionately. For a moment, she was lost in him, feeling the heat of his body against hers. If she would have been in a more private spot, she would have thrown him down and made wild love to him, but she could hear people on the street, and she pulled back, frowning. "No. I love you, but we've got to stop."

"I don't want to stop," he said, resting his forehead against hers. "I want to take you, and make you my mate."

"You already have a mate," Mila whispered, pulling away. Tears rushed down her face.

"I know." Anguish filled his voice as he looked at what he could not have.

"If my brother hurts you, I promise I'll kill him. We've got to figure out what he is up to," Alex said, brushing a few strands of her hair that had come loose behind her ear.

"Keep an eye on him. He'll have to go with Sadie, I expect. What will they do about their egg? It's due to hatch soon."

"So, whatever he's up to will probably happen soon. Normally, a female would ask a relative who had set an egg to keep hers warm while she left the caves. I doubt Sadie would ask Dahlia. Perhaps a friend . . . ," he thought, his mind whirling.

"She is close with Penny. I bet you she asks her. Penny has an egg." Mila gave him a sad look and pulled him out of the alley. He walked her to the door, looking at her longingly as she gave him a little wave.

"Goodbye, my love," he whispered, and then turned and walked back to the castle. No one noticed a dragon walked in their midst, or even that the plain clothed man was Crown Prince Alex of Dumara. He slipped into the crowd unseen.

Inside the shop, Kiera and Sam were gushing over the clock, and Aswin sat on a stool, looking delighted at the sound the dragon made at the top of the hour. It lifted its carved head and gave out a musical roar. Aswin looked up at Mila as she walked in and noted the look of distress on her face. "Alex said he had something to discuss with you. He told me about Nick's visit. I trust you two talked?"

"Yes, we did. He said he would kill his brother if he ever harmed me." She slid onto the stool next to her father, looking at the clock. She traced the figure of the dragon with her finger. It was obviously a sunrise dragon, red like King Rand. The one on the other was carved in oak and had the golden tone of Alex. Obviously, a coincidence, but she loved it. "This is a beautiful clock."

Her father looked at her oddly. Something was obviously up with Mila and Alex, but if she didn't want to talk about it, he could take the hint. He pulled out the list that Mila had left in the till and pondered.

He opened up his mind's connection with King Rand. He was bound to him, and they shared the same connection that Alex and Mila shared. "What could your son want with these things?" he thought.

"I don't know, but he's up to no good. I'm going to have Alex try to follow him the next time he goes out. We'll get to the bottom of this. Alex came to me today and told me he didn't like my idea of sending Nick to Norda. He thinks it's a bad idea, and that Nick will refuse, but I don't have any other option. I've got to try," Rand thought to him from the throne room in the castle. Aswin could tell he was holding court, because he could hear in the background a farmer talking about losing his crop to a blight and begging the King for a bit of gold to get back on his feet.

"I'll let you get back to it. I'll let you know if anything else comes up," Aswin said, and then put down the list with a sigh.

CHAPTER 5

RELATIONSHIPS

The following day, Alex lumbered out of his nest, cranky and tired. He had been up all night, pondering his dilemma with Mila. Dahlia slept next to him, content and unaware his heart ached for another. As he slipped out of the nest, Dahlia turned a worried eye to him. "Where are you going?"

"Don't worry about it." he snapped at her, and she turned away, with hurt in her eyes. She knew something had been bothering him lately and thought it was probably his difficulties with his brother. He had been short with her, and never wanted to touch her since she had set an egg. She supposed this was her life, and what she signed up for when she agreed to a loveless marriage with the Crown Prince.

She had been hoping he would stay close today, with their egg. She trusted Sadie as far as she could throw her. There was no way she would leave her egg with that wretch of a drakaina lurking close by. She would have to ask her friend Rose, if she could find her, if Rose would watch her egg. It had been days since she had gone out, and she needed to stretch her wings.

Down the hall, Sadie and Nick were conspiring. Their heads close together, they whispered to each other.

"I need to go home for a few days, Nick. The dragons will fly any day now, and I must greet the summer," she pleaded.

"I'm in the middle of something, Sadie. I can't just stop what I'm doing to watch our egg!" he protested. "I'm planning on heading to Fresthav and Murdad. I've got a date in mind, and I'll need their forces to subdue the clan."

"When is your date, love?" Sadie asked, twinning her neck around his and caressing him gently with her claws.

He couldn't resist Sadie, he never could. He felt his lust rising and roared. She chuckled and lowered herself into the submissive pose.

"You don't know what you do to me, Sadie," he said, being careful to push the bronze-colored egg to the side.

"Then let me fly. I'll be back soon," she whispered, looking at him with her orange eyes.

"Fine," he roared, and then moved to take her.

———

Dahlia picked up her egg gently with her mouth, wrapping her tongue around it. She then lumbered down the hall and delivered it to her friend, Rose.

Rose was a dark red dragon, deep red like the summer blooms, hence the name. Dahlia and she had been friends since they were dragonlings.

Rose and her mate Chain were expecting as well. Their egg was a unique pink color. Dahlia gently set her egg in Rose's nest.

"Thank you for looking after this for me. I worry Sadie will try to harm it. She's so jealous our son will be the heir."

"She's a blight," declared Rose. "I can't stand her and her little group of friends. She thinks she is superior to us, because she's a summer dragon. She just waltzed in here with her green self like she owns the place, bossing us all around like she's the Queen. If Alex ever takes the crown, she will be in for a bad day."

"I know, Rose. She's not my favorite either. The brief time we shared a family cave was just the worst. Thank goodness Alex and I have our own cave now," Dahlia said.

"How are things between you?" Rose asked, looking at her friend carefully. She sensed Dahlia was hiding something.

"It's great. Just great," she said, more brightly than she felt.

"Come on, Dahlia. I know you. You don't look happy."

"Well," she said carefully, "You know we didn't marry for love. At first, he was very attentive, eager to start a family. Now that we have the egg, it's like he's forgotten about me. I've been lonely."

"I'm sorry, Dahlia. I'm sure this is all just post-egg adjustment. After your dragonling is hatched, things will be different," Rose said, looking at her friend tenderly.

"Yeah, you're probably right. Alex has had a lot on his mind, with his brother causing problems and everything."

"Go, get a nice flight in, visit the girls. Your egg is safe with me," Rose said, smiling and showing her sharp teeth.

"Thank you, Rose. I appreciate it," Dahlia said, slipping out into the hallway. She made straight for the entrance and launched herself out, flying for the first time in weeks. Oh, it felt so good. She stretched her wings out wide and then turned to the south. Maybe she would fly down to the point and catch a few seals.

With a happy roar, she called to any clan dragons who were nearby to join her, and she was quickly joined by two younger females, who were unmated, and therefore happy to go hunting with her.

———

After Sadie had given Nick her attention this morning, he had slipped into sleep. She quickly stole out of the nest and made her way to the entrance. She sniffed the air and discovered that it was indeed still winter. After the summer dragons flew, the air took on a distinct smell. It was the smell of dirt, and of the sun. Spring smelled glorious. She could tell they were right on the edge of it, though, and she would have to hurry home to make it in time.

A few dragons gave her the side eye, wondering what she was doing sniffing the air. They wouldn't understand. They were sunrise dragons; they performed their duties every day. Her clan only had half of the year. They brought forth the summer in the spring, and then periodically throughout the season, flew across the continent, bestowing their magic to the lands below. Without the summer dragons, crops would not thrive, birds and insects would not multiply, and animals would not grow fat for the winter.

She launched herself into the air, immediately turning east. She would fly a more southerly route, over Sunrise Bay and the Bay of Terrek. She didn't want to run into nightfall dragons on her own. As far as she knew, relations between Murdad and Terrek were still tense, as her father had signed an agreement with Dumara.

Ahhh, but it felt good to fly. It had been sometime since she had been out. Soon though, their egg would hatch, and she would meet their dragonling. Born of both light and flame, their little one would be so powerful. It was like a little miracle. And one day, he would be united in marriage with the daughter of the Queen of Fresthav, and their children would be ice and fire, light and dark, and rule the world.

It was a long flight, but she enjoyed the views below. The peaceful rolling hills of Dumara below her, with scattered farm holdings, and then once she reached Terrek's shores, the tidy ranch lands, filled with immense herds of animals. She didn't realize how much she had missed home until she saw the four towers of Terrek rising out of the crater. Her heart leapt as she saw dragons in every shade of green, flying in and out of their subterranean caves.

She quickly swooped into the cave, feeling its dark coolness. She could hear the chatter before she even felt the hard stone under her claws.

"It's Princess Sadie! She's come!" the voices muttered.

"I am here. Where is Tyson?" she demanded.

"We will call for him!" A drakaina said, and then roared loudly. Soon, the caves were full of voices rising, all calling for Tyson.

In a few minutes, Tyson appeared with his young son trailing behind.

"Sadie! I was wondering if you were going to join us. Your father plans on greeting the summer in just a few days."

"I am here, Dragon Keeper. Is my family upstairs? If they are, change me, I desire to see them immediately," she demanded.

"Of course," he said, pulling out a bottle of astragenica from the bag slung over his shoulder. Causally, he pulled the cork off, and then poured the contents into her maw.

She began to change, and she relished it. It had been months since she had taken her human form. The last time she had walked on two legs had been her wedding day. She didn't really have any reason to go upstairs in Dumara, and her husband preferred his dragon form. She felt her front legs shorten and her claws retract. Her back legs changed next, and then she felt her whole body shrinking into itself.

She lifted her head and stared into the face of the small boy. Tyson's son, Michael, grinned and handed her a simple dress from the clothing they kept nearby. It was probably her mother's, but it would do.

"Thank you, young man," she said, slipping it over her head.

"Come, Sadie. Your parents will be happy to see you and hear your news. They've missed you," Tyson said, offering her his arm.

Together, they walked to the ascender, and she listened to young Michael tell her about all his adventures with his father. She smiled and patted him on the head. "You're a good boy, helping your father so much. Make sure you pay attention, for one day, his job will be yours."

He nodded, his eyes shining brightly.

———

Darius Fletcher, sorcerer of Dumara, sat with arm around Gayle, next to a stream that ran by his tower. She had still not left him, even though it had been nearly a week since she had arrived.

Linnea had left after the first day, telling her to contact her mother when she wanted a return ride home.

Thora was angry Gayle was not back yet, but Gayle had made sure to leave a large amount of supplies with her new assistant, so the dragons of Fresthav were cared for.

Darius grabbed his staff from where it lay next to him. He considered a clump of green. "Erupit FLOS!" he said, giving force and power to the words. His staff shone brightly, and blue power surrounded the leaves. Suddenly, the bush sprang into bud and then transitioned to bloom. Three perfectly formed purple meadow flowers, dripping with a cloying scent, formed in front of their eyes.

Gayle looked at the bush with wonder. He leaned over, picked one, and tucked it behind her ear.

He kissed her forehead and sighed. "I don't want you to leave," he said simply.

"How do you do that? That's amazing," she whispered, looking at him with huge eyes.

"I have the magic of the Dragon God. I can do pretty much anything. It has consequences, though. This bush won't bloom again until next year. I pushed its life force forward. It will die back early this year and won't bloom again until next. A small problem, but think if I did that on a big scale. Magic can be dangerous."

"Kind of like the life potion you gave me for Thora?" she asked.

"I must do magic to make that. You could replicate the herbs, but you would be missing the magic. It's a curse really. I wish I had never made that deal with Erza, and then I would still be living in Dumara, toiling in complete ignorance as a shopkeeper."

"But then we would never have met. I don't want to leave, but I must. Queen Thora has sent Linnea back to pick me up. She will be here in a few hours."

"I love you, Gayle. I've only loved one other person, and that went badly."

"I know," she said. He had opened his heart to her, something

44

she had a feeling he had rarely done before. "This has been an amazing week."

"What was your favorite part?" he asked, teasing. "My cooking or my prowess in bed?"

"Well, it definitely wasn't your cooking," she giggled. He was a terrible cook. She had taken over after two days of beans, finding some nice greens growing in the nearby meadow, while she hunted a rabbit for their dinner. She had roasted it with a bit of wine and wild garlic.

Besides cooking and making love, they had worked together in his workshop. He had shown her things he had never shown another soul, about magic, spells, and veta stones. Not that she could use them, lacking the blessing of the Dragon God, but she had been mesmerized by his knowledge, asking him questions and surprised to get answers from the notoriously cagey sorcerer.

"You're amazing. When can I see you again?" he asked, playing with her long dark locks. She looked at him sadly. "I don't know, Queen Thora isn't going to be happy I've been gone so long. It will be a while before I can get away."

"What if I come to see you?" he asked, smiling. He rarely left his tower, but he might do it, for this woman.

"I guess that would work. I can show you my workshop! It's a bit tidier than yours!" she giggled, burying her head into his shoulder. This last week, she had helped him clean up his workshop. And by help, she stood on the sidelines and directed him what to do next. He found that once decades of trash had been cleaned up, his potions and herbs organized, he liked it. He doubted he could keep it tidy for long. He just didn't have an organized bone in his body.

"You're good for me, Gayle. I'll come visit, as soon as I can. I might have to hitch a ride on a sunrise dragon, or buy a horse. But I promise, I'll come."

She smiled at him and gave him a kiss. "I would like that, Darius."

———

Sadie was greeted by her parents in their parlor. Her mother and father sat together on the long sofa. Her brother was upstairs, studying with his tutor. At 14, he still had a few years before he would be done with his studies.

"Ahhh, my daughter returns," Cleon said, looking at her coldly.

"Oh, my dear, it's so good to see you," Shayla said, clapping her hands in delight. "We will have to have a party tonight! We will have music, and dancing, and we'll get the chef to make us a special dinner. I've missed you so, my daughter." Shayla stood, giving her daughter a warm hug, and then sat next to her on the opposite sofa.

"Hello parents. I sensed that it was almost time to greet the summer. I wanted to come," she said, simply, looking at her father.

"It's good you've not completely forgotten your clan or your duties," he said with bitterness.

"I've set an egg. You're going to be grandparents soon. Our son will hatch within the month."

Her mother looked worried, glancing at her husband, whose mouth was set in a thin line. Cleon picked up a decanter of iseiki and poured himself a glass. He took a big drink and didn't look at his daughter again. "Have you heard it, Sadie? The beating of the drums? Once a week, I hear two distinct beats. It's a warning from the Dragon God. I heard the news that your wedding was not blessed. If you continue this path, we are all doomed."

"Father. The wedding was a bit of a disaster, I'll admit. That sorcerer Darius is incompetent. His staff merely wasn't functioning properly. That is all. Dumara is prone to earthquakes, just a coincidence. And the sorcerer tried to cover for his ineptitude by causing us to hear voices and attributing it to the supernatural. But I assure you, Nick and I are married."

"But at what cost, daughter?" Cleon said, taking another deep drink. "Well, I am glad to see you. Since you are here now, and probably desire to return to your egg, we will move up greeting the summer. It's just about time anyway. We will ride tomorrow. I'll let Tyson know. He'll probably want to bring his son. I guess he can ride Kip."

"Now, tell me about your egg, you're sure it's a son?" Shayla said, delighted. She would have to pay a visit to Dumara to meet her grandson as soon as he made an appearance. She might have to talk Cleon into it. He hated to leave Terrek.

"It's a lovely bronze color, mother. I think he will be a beautiful princeling. And of course, we are delighted it's a son. He will be the Crown Prince, once Nick takes the throne," she said, forgetting herself.

Her father's eyebrows raised. "That's a bit presumptive, isn't it? Alex is the Crown Prince."

Sadie gulped. "Well, you know, if something should happen to Alex. Dahlia and he do not have an heir, yet." She was still scheming about how she could crush Dahlia's egg when the opportunity presented itself. Dahlia couldn't watch it forever. She would have to go out at some point. And if she slipped, then all the better.

Cleon shook his head, disturbed by her attitude. King Rand was a good friend, and if he was being honest, he would have been much happier if Sadie and Crown Prince Alex would have married. He had never liked Nick. The boy was sneaky, and he was not to be trusted.

"We have news to share also. Your brother has been betrothed. He will marry Flora when he turns eighteen. We are pushing it a little, of course, but it was the only way to appease the clan after you left."

"I'll make sure to give him my regards," Sadie said evenly, wondering how the clan would treat her tomorrow, when they flew together.

———

After spending a lovely night with her family, downstairs in the family nest, laughing and talking as if she had never left, she joined the clan as they lined up at the entrance. Tyson was there, with his son Michael, who was nearly bursting with excitement, his eyes wide with anticipation.

The dragons, huge and lumbering, shifted and moved in a large group, roaring in their own excitement. Tyson helped Michael up on Kip, who turned his dark green head and looked at the young boy with his vibrant green eyes. Michael wrapped his hands into Kip's black mane, delight on his face. "Take care of my boy, Kip."

"Don't worry, Tyson. I'll make sure he doesn't fall off." Kip laughed. "Don't pull so hard, kid."

"What did he say?" Michael shouted. He wouldn't become bound to Kip until he reached the age of 18, and then they could mentally communicate.

"He said don't pull so hard," Tyson said, as he chuckled. He remembered his first ride on Cleon, when he was still the Crown Prince, many, many years ago. It was a rite of passage.

Cleon was next to him, waiting patiently. Tyson swung up on the dark green dragon effortlessly, patting his head. Cleon snorted, his nostrils flaring. He shook his head, and his black mane flew out in all directions. He turned his orange eyes and looked at his clan. As their King, he would announce the coming of summer. He roared, tilting his head straight up, his flames igniting and flowing out of his nose, twenty feet in the air. All around him, the other summer dragons followed, and the caves were alight with noise and heat.

With a mighty roar, Cleon jumped into the sky, twirling in a perfect spiral as he headed straight into the air, flames all around him as he lit up the morning sky. Behind him, nearly two hundred dragons followed. The sound and heat was overwhelming.

Michael was scared, and he was holding on as hard as he could. He closed his eyes as his stomach dropped out from under him. The heat from the flames was almost uncomfortable, and he started to sweat in his cloak.

48

Next to her brother, Sadie joined in the celebration, happy to be a part of this tradition. She had been right to worry. The summer dragons ignored her solidly, not even returning her greetings this morning. When she tried to talk to old friends, she got the cold shoulder. It was apparent they were angry with her, but she took solace that at least her family still welcomed her home.

The bodies of the dragons were a shifting sea of green scales. Teal, chartreuse, kelly, lime, hunter, mint, light green, jade, and emerald. Every shade combined to form an impressive sight.

They turned due east, roaring and blowing their smoke and fire every few minutes. They lit up the sky, and the people below ran out to welcome them. The flight of the summer dragons was a yearly event. Tonight, the small towns across the continent would host impromptu town fairs. They would light bonfires, symbolizing the coming of spring and warmth. For all, the flight of the summer dragons meant that the long hard winter was over. It was time to prepare the fields and get ready for the bounty of summer.

Sadie felt at peace as she flew. This is where she belonged, not with the sunrise dragons who only befriended her because of to whom she was married. After a few hours they flew past Dumara. They were greeted by a few sunrise dragons who watched their passing, greeting her by name.

They flew on to Fresthav, and this is where you could really see their magic at work. As they flew, they brought sunshine and warmth to the frozen land below. The snow melted under them, and soon they reached the frozen capitol of Fresthav, the city covered with frost and ice.

As always, they could never completely unfreeze the city below. There were simply too many winter dragons in the vicinity. But the winter dragons accepted their season was over and roared their greetings as they passed.

Next was the trickiest part of the trip, the flight over Murdad. They would not be challenged, as they did not challenge the nightfall dragons when they were performing their sacred duties of greeting the moon, but they would not exactly be welcomed, either.

49

They flew over the dead plains, flying south of the city of Murdad, tucked at the base of a fearsome volcano that poured lava all year round. The nightfall dragons lived inside the volcano, residing in the obsidian caves that pocketed the mountain.

They only saw nightfall dragons from a distance, and when the nightfall dragons spotted them, the purple dragons turned immediately home, avoiding the summer dragons at all costs.

Soon, they reached the western edge of the continent, and turned to the south, flying over the Great Divide and bound for home.

One by one, they landed in the caves. It was the end of the day, and they were all exhausted and thoroughly spent. Even Michael had struggled to stay awake on the last leg, finally resting his head in the mane of Kip. He awoke as they landed, and he slipped off the back of Kip as soon as he could, sore and tired.

He watched his father quickly start administering astragenica to the royal family, one after the other. He hurried to be of help, gathering their clothes and distributing them.

Kip changed, and then knelt next to the tired boy, ruffling his hair. "You did good, boy. You'll make a fine Dragon Keeper one day."

Sadie turned into her human form quickly. All of her clan mates avoided looking at her. Feeling sad, she turned with her family to head up to the ascender. She would rest tonight and then leave first thing tomorrow. She had to get back to her egg and her husband. The dragons of summer had thoroughly rejected her today, and she felt sad she was no longer a part of this world. She would have to build her own world now, and her and Nick would make it to their liking.

CHAPTER 6

THE PLOT

Sadie had arrived back, and she had taken her place in their nest. The past few days she had been quiet, and she had slept for hours and hours.

"What's wrong, love?" Nick said, nuzzling her shoulder.

"My visit didn't go well. I was expecting a warmer welcome."

"They did not treat you well?" he said, his hackles rising.

"They just ignored me for the most part," she said sadly, looking at her beautiful bronze egg. "There seems to be some animosity toward me."

"Soon, Sadie. We will rule, and they will ignore us no longer," Nick said dangerously. Just then, one of Sadie's friends slunk into the room. Teeta, a long golden dragon with a red stripe down her back approached. "You asked for me?"

"Yes. I have to go on an errand with my husband. I want you to watch my egg while I'm gone," Sadie said, not looking at her.

"I would be honored, but why do you not ask Dahlia?" Teeta wondered.

Sadie hissed. "She does not leave her egg with me, so I do not leave mine with her. We are not close, even though we are related by marriage."

"Oh," Teeta said, looking around. She was an unmated dragon, and didn't have her own egg or her own nest.

"You can stay here, in our nest. We will only be gone a day. If anything happens to this egg, I promise you, this will be the last task you ever do," Nick said, growling.

"Nick, be nice to Teeta. She's a good friend of mine. She will show our egg the same love and care we do," Sadie admonished him, slipping out of the nest with Nick.

"Of course," Teeta said, taking the still warm spot and wrapping herself around the bronze egg. "It is a pleasure and a privilege."

Nick and Sadie made for the entrance, and he began to roar for the Dragon Keeper. Aswin was down several levels, working with Mila on caring for the elderly dragon Sall.

"Ugh. I think Nick wants us. I hear his roar. I'd better hurry up. You know how he gets if he has to wait," Aswin said, grabbing his bag and hurrying out. "I'll leave you here."

"Sure, Father," Mila said. She was sitting at Sall's head, stroking his long white mane. He was in a lot of pain, suffering from rheumatism. She had given him a tonic to reduce inflammation, and he was resting easier now, but it was hard for him to move around. She picked up a chunk of raw meat and held it out to him.

"Here, Sall. Eat. You haven't eaten for days," she said.

"It's hard for me to walk upstairs, and my son has been busy with other things," Sall said sadly. He gently took the raw meat from her hand with his teeth and gulped it down with one bite.

Mila started to sing him a song while rubbing his nose. His eyes got heavier and heavier, and soon he was snoring lightly. She smiled and got up, brushing her pants off. She picked up her bag and headed back up the hallway toward the entrance.

She met her father halfway back. "I took care of Sall, he's sleeping now. What did Nick want?"

"It was actually Sadie. She wanted to be changed. She headed upstairs to get something she forgot. I think they are going somewhere."

Just then, Alex reached out to her and spoke through their shared thoughts. "My brother is being sneaky again. I think he's going somewhere. I just saw him and Sadie leave, and Sadie was human and carrying a bag. I bet she's got those potions with her. Come upstairs, Mila. We are going to follow them."

She turned to her father, "Alex wants to shadow them. We will be leaving now. I think we are done down here, although you might want to check on Little Shriek, the dragonling had that cough yesterday."

"I will do so. But please be careful, Mila. Who knows what Nick is up to, and what danger he will lead you into," her father said, his forehead creased with worry.

"Don't worry about me, Dad. Alex will take care of me." She hurried back to the entrance with her Dragon Keeper's bag. Alex was already standing at the opening, his dragon wings rustling with impatience. Without a word, she swung on, and they launched off the ledge.

"There he is, to the north. I can just make them out!" Alex said, flapping his wings rhythmically to gain speed.

Mila shielded her eyes from the sun. If she squinted, she could just make out the speck in the distance. "I see them. You think they are headed to Murdad?"

"That's the only place in the north," Alex said grimly.

"Well, let's see what he's up to," Mila said, holding her bag tight. She hadn't had time to belt it on.

They sped northwards, closing the distance, but trying to keep far enough behind so they would not be spotted.

Nick was indeed headed to Murdad, and now Mila could see Sadie on his back, her black hair flying free. As they approached the Great Divide, clouds started to build.

"Hades," Alex swore. "We're going to lose them in those storm clouds. Looks like a spring thunderstorm."

And indeed, a minute later, Nick and Sadie disappeared into the thick, dark, swirling mist. Thunder rumbled in the distance, and flashes of light lit up the clouds.

The stormfront towered up to great heights. There would be no way they could fly over it, but it looked like it was just a string of storms. Beyond a strip of dark shadows on the ground, they could see bright shining sunlight. "I think we will just punch through. We'll get a little wet, but we should be able to pick them up on the other side."

Mila laughed, "Okay, I'll put my hood up." She did, and Alex dove into the thunderstorm.

The rain hit her like a brick wall, cold as ice and drenching her almost immediately. She was glad her bag was mostly waterproof. She held her breath as lightning struck all around her. Alex wasn't worried about it for some reason, so she tried not to be as well. Through the blinding rain, she could see the mountain tops below her, dark and craggy.

In just a minute, they had punched through the other side, and the land of Murdad lay below them. Mila could see silver mines below her, with the wretched humans Murdad enslaved toiling hard.

All of the sudden, she heard an evil laugh, and from above them, something red flashed. She saw claws outstretched, and she felt a glancing blow.

She tried to hold on, but the blow hit her so hard she must have been knocked senseless for a moment, and then she was tumbling through the air, a handful of golden mane still in her fingers.

"MILA!" Alex roared, twisting away. HIs brother, Nick made a hard left to the west, laughing evilly. "I never liked her!" Nick roared as he shot back into the clouds.

Alex had only seconds to act. He dove, tucking his wings in.

Mila was tumbling through the air, terrified, the wind on her face as she watched the ground quickly get closer and closer. She was going to die. Nick had knocked her off his brother's back on purpose.

She had lost her bag, and she closed her eyes hoping for a quick death.

Alex would not let that happen. His claws outstretched, he quickly grabbed her body, his claws wrapping around her. She stopped falling, but the impact of his claws knocked the wind out of her. His claws were around her middle and her legs, and the impact of him stopping tossed her like a rag doll. He quickly turned back to the south. He would have to find somewhere in friendly territory to put her down and assess her injuries.

Mila was likely knocked unconscious, because Alex wasn't able to open their mind connection. With great fear, he flew as fast as he could back over the mountains and through the rainstorm, hoping against hope that she wasn't dead in his claws.

He found an island he knew about, in the middle of Lake Cypress. The waterfall to the north bubbled angrily with the addition of the rainstorm. As gently as possible, he put her down on the island. She slipped out of his claws onto the ground, and he landed beside her.

Mila awoke to pain, and to Alex licking her face. "Stop!" she gasped. His tongue was dry and scratchy like sandpaper. She laughed, and pain grabbed her ribs. She held them and moaned. Everywhere was painful.

"Mila! Are you hurt? Oh god, I was so scared," Alex said, worriedly looking over her with concern.

"Everywhere hurts," she moaned. "My ribs, my legs."

"I had to grab you with my claws. Did I cut you?" he said, terrified. He didn't see any blood.

"I don't know. I don't think so," she said, taking stock. She managed to sit up, and she looked down at herself. "I don't' see any blood, but I think I'm badly bruised. Better than dead, I guess." She tried to laugh again, and pain shot threw her side. "Maybe some busted up ribs? I've lost my bag somewhere. This is terrible."

"My brother deliberately tried to kill you," Alex said, his voice grumbling deeply. "I'm going to make him pay."

Mila looked at him in fear. "Why would he do that? Doesn't he know you will go to your father?"

"He wanted to lose us, which he obviously did. He had business in Murdad. I'm going to take this to my father. Nick is a traitor, and we will get to the bottom of it."

"What do you think your father will do?" Mila asked, standing up. She noticed that the thick sturdy material of her pants were torn into shreds from Alex's claws, and her thighs were already turning interesting colors. She was badly bruised and sore. She slowly walked toward him and laid her head on his side.

"I think he'll send him away. The farther the better," Alex said. "Do you feel well enough to ride? I want to get you home, and speak to my father, as soon as possible."

"Yeah," Mila said, "But I might be a minute trying to climb on."

"Here, this may help." Alex lowered himself onto the ground, so his belly was fully flat on the earth. He lowered his head also. Mila gingerly was able to swing her body up on his back, moaning as the pain in her limbs settled in. "I wish I hadn't lost my bag, I could have whipped up a painkiller."

"I can feel your pain in my mind, and it angers me. My brother is going to pay," Alex said.

Mila patted his head and noticed a bare patch where she had torn out his hair when she had been knocked off. "I'm afraid you are missing a big patch of your mane here. Sorry."

"I barely felt it. The important thing is that I managed to grab you." As gently as possible, he rose into the air, and headed back as quickly as possible to Dumara.

———

Sadie was on the back of Nick. "Do you think she's dead? Maybe we should swing back around and find her body."

"I don't care. Either she is, or she isn't. We've got a meeting in Murdad to make," Nick said, quickening his pace.

"Your brother is going to tell your father," Sadie said, looking back over her shoulder. She had lost sight of Alex, and she felt anxiety rising in her breast.

"I'll just tell him it was an accident. I lost my way in the storm, flew too far north, and accidentally ran into him." Nick shrugged under her.

"I don't know Nick. Do you think your father will believe that?" Sadie asked, concerned.

"It doesn't matter. By tomorrow night, he will be dead, and I'll be King. The plan is in motion. All the men in Dumara are waiting for me to act."

The volcano of Murdad appeared in the distance, glowing red with the lava that spilled down its slopes. The imposing fortress, made of black pumice, rose out of the desolate plains. In the town, factories run by men belched thick choking smoke into the sky. A dirty black river, filled with coal ash, snaked underneath them, and sorry looking huts dotted the landscape. Small herds of scrawny looking goats ate sagebrush and scrub. Each small homestead had small plots of nox beans, a small bitter bean that was the staple of the people who lived here, protected by rickety wooden fencing.

Nick had obviously been to Murdad before, and he flew to the volcano directly. Sadie was surprised no one challenged them, but maybe they were expecting him.

She ducked as they flew into a small hole. On the interior it opened into a large room, in which a river of lava ran. A very tall and muscular man stood glaring at them with unnaturally yellow eyes, dressed all in black with silver accents on his clothes.

"Welcome, traitor. My father waits to speak to you," Kai Monserrat, Crown Prince of Murdad said in his deep voice. Doyle, the Dragon Keeper, shuffled forward.

"I brought our own potions." Sadie said, slipping off and reaching into her bag for the astragenica they had demanded from Mila, who now probably lay broken on the Dead Plains.

"Don't trust an old man, ehhh?" Doyle chuckled, crossing his arms and watching her closely.

Nick changed, and Sadie handed him a black shirt and pants.

With a grin, he put them on quickly, and then offered her his arm. "Come dear, Ibis awaits."

All four headed upstairs, to the throne room of the King of Murdad.

Ibis was trying to make an impression. He had 200 troops, lined up in full armor, holding their long pole arms. He was sitting on his throne, set with purple veta stones, and wearing a silver crown, each point set with a large veta stone. He looked bored as they walked toward him.

"Father, Prince Nick of Dumara is here, as previously arranged," Kai said, giving his father a smart bow. Nick watched the King closely. His eyes flicked toward Sadie.

"Sadie Dayia. Former Princess of Terrek. How lovely to see you today. Has your dragonling arrived yet?" he said in a gravelly voice, his eyes glinting.

"Not yet. Very soon, our son will be born," Sadie said, clutching her husband's arm. She didn't like this man, for he oozed evil.

"Ahhh, my granddaughter in Fresthav has already arrived. One day, our children will marry, and take over this world. What a glorious day that will be," he said, looking at the window.

"All the clans shall be united as one, under one rule," Nick said, his voice swelling with pride.

"Yes, but until then, is the little matter of Dumara. They vex me so," Ibis said, tracing the decoration on the arm of his chair.

"I've come today to tell you the plan is in motion. By tomorrow night, my father and brother will be dead, and I will be King. The nightfall dragons will arrive to help me subdue the clan?"

"Yes, we will arrive. You promise inside help?"

"Yes, I have twenty sunrise dragons who support me in the caves. With your reinforcements, we will crush any opposition."

"And there will be opposition. It won't take long for the clan to figure out you've killed your father and brother to take the throne," Ibis said, looking into the Prince's eyes. So naive. Nick thought he would take the throne so easily. Ibis knew it wouldn't be easy, but it was possible, especially with help from Fresthav and Murdad.

"Of course, but they will see my might. Once my brother is gone, and his egg crushed, I will be the only Chuvash remaining. They will have to accept me," Nick said, his eyes filled with the promise of power.

"Yes, they will," Ibis said, and he turned to his general who was standing stiffly nearby. "General Atum, start preparing for war. We will fly out the day after tomorrow, dragons with riders, to Dumara. You will take orders from Nick here, and you will help secure the city for him. Our dragons will secure the caves."

"Yes, sir. Of course, we will be ready to ride at your command," General Atum said, giving his liege a short bow.

"If you see the black flag on the ramparts flying, you know the King is dead and I've seized power. And now, I must ride. I make for Fresthav, to tell them of our plans. They will send forces also," Nick said, turning to leave.

"That's a long trip. Can you make it after already flying here today?" Kai said, looking over Nick.

"I can make it, don't worry about me," Nick growled, low in his throat.

"Okay, okay. Just didn't want our plan to fall apart before it started."

"My plan is flawless. We won't fail," Nick said, leaving the room, with Sadie at his heels.

———

Alex landed in the caves and Mila slipped off. He bellowed for Aswin urgently, and the message was passed. He quickly arrived, concern on his face. "What is it, Alex?" He knew Alex only called him urgently if there was an actual problem.

"Mila's hurt. It's a long story, but my brother knocked her off, and I caught her midair. She's a bit bruised and battered," Alex said, anger in his voice.

"Nick did what?" Aswin said, staring at Alex in confusion.

"You heard me. He willfully tried to kill Mila. I need to talk to my father."

"I've lost my bag, Father. I'm sorry," Mila said, tears squeezing from her eyes. She hurt all over, and the emotions of the day were catching up with her.

"No worries, Mila. A bag can be replaced, but you are priceless." Aswin turned, holding up an astragenica potion. Alex nodded, holding his mouth open. Aswin poured it in, and soon Alex stood before them.

Realizing that Mila had lost the clothes she had stuffed in her bag, he went over to the storage chest and dug around until he found a tunic. "This will have to do. I need to talk to my father."

"Alex, maybe he didn't mean to try to kill me," Mila said, second-guessing herself.

"Go home, Mila. I'll see you tomorrow. Rest well," Alex said, turning toward the stairway that led up to the castle.

"We will go up with you. I don't know if she's up for a trek down that path," Aswin said, moving to his daughter's side. She walked gingerly, holding her ribs in pain.

They left Alex in the main hall, and then made their way to the gatehouse. Soon, they were home.

Sam looked up as they came into the shop. He took one look at Mila and said, "What happened?"

He was checking out a customer, Old Maid Riley, who turned to Mila with her mouth wide open. "Mila Fletcher, you look terrible. Really, you should stay home. It's unseemly for you to be gallivanting around on dragons like you do."

"Good day to you, Ms. Riley," Mila said curtly, moving to sit down gingerly on her chair. Ms. Riley left the shop, and her father turned the sign to closed.

"Mila's lost her bag, Sam. I think I've got an old beat up one down in the basement. It was the first bag I used. We can set that up for her until I can have another one made."

"Could I get a pain powder?" Mila asked. A bag was all fine

and good, but she felt terrible. She wanted to take a hot bath and go to bed.

"Yes, of course," Sam said, turning and grabbing a few packets of ground willow bark and handing them to Mila.

"Come, Mila. I want to see your injuries," her father said, leading her upstairs. "Sam, close up the shop for the day." Her father led Mila upstairs to the bath, turning it on. He turned around while she took off her clothes and slipped on her robe. She sat on the edge of the bath and pulled up the edge of her robe so they could look at her thighs. Angry purple and black bruises covered her legs.

"My ribs are just as black," she groaned.

"Well, it's a wonder Alex managed to grab you," her father said, fear coming into his voice. He realized just then that Mila could be dead. He didn't know if he could stand to lose her also.

"I'll be fine, I just need to heal," Mila said.

"I'll make this willow bark tea for you while your bath is filling."

"Thanks, Dad," she said. In a few minutes, her father brought her a tray, with a mug of hot tea and a sandwich.

He left to go make his own dinner, and she slipped into the hot water, drinking the bitter tea. She felt better already. The warmth and the medicine pulled the pain from her limbs, and she felt herself drifting off.

She awoke with a start, with her bathwater growing cold, realizing that Alex and King Rand were having a heated conversation. She could hear it in her mind. She paid attention as she pulled the plug on her bathwater, and then wrapped herself in a towel and her robe. She slipped into bed, in the dark, listening intently.

———

"It wasn't an accident, Father. Nick legitimately tried to kill Mila. I don't know why. Out of jealousy, anger, or something else. He knocked her off, and laughed as she fell. I realized today he is a psychopath, and he doesn't care who he hurts. He only cares about himself," Alex said, looking at his father over their dinner.

Nick had still not returned, and Alex was worried as to what he was up to.

Rand looked like the weight of the world was on his shoulders. "What do you think he and Sadie were up to in Murdad?"

"Who knows? But he was obviously going to Murdad, with Sadie, astragenica, and energy potions. He would turn into his human form. Perhaps to meet someone, maybe even King Monserrat. He's got two energy potions, so he could easily fly to Fresthav and back tonight. I don't trust him, he's plotting something," Alex said.

"Your brother is just playing a game. I trust he has our best interests at heart. But he shouldn't be meeting Murdad and Fresthav without talking to us," Rand said, shaking his head. He would not believe his son was a traitor. There had to be a reason for this. Nick must be trying to gather information.

"Father, why don't you see what is in front of your face? He tried to kill Mila, doesn't that count for anything?" Alex was getting angry, his face was flushed. "If I hadn't grabbed her, she would have died. I couldn't live with myself. . . ." His voice broke, and tears sprang from his eyes.

Rand paused, a bite of his chicken halfway between his plate and his mouth. "Oh. You love her, don't you?" he said softly.

Alex wiped his mouth with a napkin, nodding his head. He couldn't speak the words, but it was evident on his grief-filled face.

Rand sighed. "I'm sorry, Alex. I made you marry Dahlia. I'm sure this has all been difficult for you, and with your dragonling on its way, you've been under a lot of stress."

"Father, my stress has nothing to do with what we are talking about. Nick is dangerous, and you need to take care of him!" He threw down his napkin and glared at his father.

"Listen, he should get back tonight. We will speak to him tomorrow morning, together. I'm going to tell him that I'm sending

Sadie and him to Norda. We have the new embassy there, and he will make the perfect ambassador."

"If you think sending him to Norda is going to solve the problem, I fear you are mistaken. He's not going to like that plan."

"It will get him out of the way. He won't be able to turn into a dragon in Norda. They don't allow dragons on the southern continent."

"Even more reason he will not want to go," Alex said bitterly. "But it's obvious I can't change your mind, Father."

———

Gayle had only been back in Fresthav three days before Darius arrived. After she had left, he gathered together his things, rode to the nearby village of Wooddale, and bought a horse and provisions.

With a grin on his face, he had set off to the east, giving Dumara a wide berth. It was early spring, and he smiled as he saw the summer dragons roar by, bringing even warmer temperatures. He took his time ambling to Fresthav, glad it wasn't so cold overnight. He camped rough and dreamed of Gayle. He realized now that he was tired of being alone, living in a cold stone tower in the middle of nowhere. If he must, he would take up residence in Fresthav so that he could be with her.

There was no way a long-distance relationship between them would work, but he was prepared to do what he had to do. He loved her, and apparently she loved him. It was quite surprising really. He wasn't going to let her slip out of his fingers.

He made his way through Vassa and then skirted the southern mountains, encountering few people. The only people he passed were on wagons loaded with timber, heading to sawmills.

In Celon, the last village before starting up the slope to Fresthav castle, he stopped and bought some sweets and a bundle of winter roses. He had promised her he might show up one day with flowers and candy, and he was making good on that promise.

———

Gayle was working in her workshop, feeling sad. When she had returned, she had been thoroughly chastised by Queen Thora for neglecting her duties. She had promised to do better, and she had given the Queen the potions, which had somewhat mollified her. The Queen was now in a deep slumber, and according to Darius, she might sleep for a month straight.

She heard a knock, and she hurried to the door. It was probably Princess Linnea, checking in with her. They were quite close, and Gayle wished she was bound to her, instead of the Queen, whose mind had been slipping more and more lately.

She opened the door and was surprised beyond words to see Darius standing there with a silly grin on his face. "I brought you flowers and candies like I promised," he said, thrusting them out at her.

She laughed and then started crying. "You came! I didn't think . . . Why . . . . Oh, my goodness!"

He set down the gifts on her table, and then swept her up in his arms. "I couldn't live without you, Gayle. I've felt more alive these past few weeks than I've felt in years. I want to be with you, if you'll have me," he said, tenderly.

"Oh, Darius. Of course. Of course, I'll have you. I love you, for some reason. You make me laugh." She kissed him and he returned her passion. It wasn't long before a trail of clothes led to her bed, and she giggled and turned off the lights.

———

A few days after Darius had arrived, he had already settled into cohabitation with Gayle. He tried to stay out of the way. Princess Linnea didn't seem to like him that much, and Gayle was usually busy most of the day in the caves. At night, they cooked together. She was teaching him how to make simple meals, and then he helped her make potions.

He did go to check on Queen Thora. Linnea was worried that she was sleeping so deeply. He pulled back her eyelid, and her eye was fully dilated, but she did not stir. He took her pulse, and it was strong and steady.

"She is fine. I told you she would sleep for some time," Darius said, looking at the wrinkled old lady sleeping in her giant bed.

"She already looks younger, and look, color is coming back into her hair," Linnea said, smoothing down her mother's long hair. Indeed, a faint ash blond color was evident at the roots.

"Well, I can't really tell, as the last time I saw Queen Thora was when she showed up with Gayle to bind her as her Dragon Keeper," Darius said, considering the Queen before him. She looked dried up, and if you hadn't told him, he would have thought she was on death's door. Apparently though, the Queen was practically indestructible. "I think with periodic potions, she would live indefinitely, but at what cost? She'll be asleep most of the time." He shook his head.

Gayle, standing beside him, grabbed his hand and shivered. "Linnea, are you sure you want to prolong her life like this?"

"This is my MOTHER you are talking about. Yes, she is fierce, but I wouldn't have it any other way. I can temper her."

They headed out of the room, and Darius decided to go down to the caves with Gayle today. He enjoyed it, even though the drakainas seemed to hate his guts. He enjoyed getting under their skin.

Gayle went to check on some of the dragonlings, and Darius tagged along. He tapped his staff on the ground. "Lux Lume," he intoned, and the stone on the top lit up with a bright light. Gayle held his hand as they walked. "What are the other clans going to do if they need you? They are going to show up at your tower, and it will be empty."

"I left a note. If they need me that badly, they can come find me in Fresthav," he said, shrugging.

The dragonling they checked on was full of energy. At about three months old, she was zipping around the nest, climbing on her mother, and sliding down her tail. Named Snowball, the young one was truly a ball of energy.

Gayle patted her little scaly white head, with its tuff of blue hair. "She is happy and healthy, Shard. Keep feeding her well, and she'll push you out of your nest in no time."

"Thank you, Dragon Keeper. Sorcerer, it is an honor to meet you today," Shard said, lowering her head to look at Darius. Her ice-blue eyes gazed at him. He had been making more of an attempt to look nicer now that he was with Gayle. His hair was trimmed, as was his beard. He looked respectable.

A roar shook the caves. "A visitor?" Gayle said, standing. "Let's go see who it is."

They made their way back down the caves. Gayle knew every twist and turn, and Darius realized he would be hopelessly lost down here in the dark. He probably could throw a directional spell to help him get out, but the thought of being in the dark alone kind of scared him.

They entered the main cave, and Darius was surprised to see the red hulk of Prince Nick, a sunrise dragon, with Sadie Dayia, in human form near him.

Nick was surrounded by winter dragons, who hissed at him. "What are YOU doing here, little princeling?" the drakainas hissed. "And you've brought this summer dragon with you, in human form. How strange."

Gayle sped forward. "Nick Chuvash. Welcome to Fresthav. I'm sorry you have not been given a warm welcome."

Sadie was just putting the astragenica in his mouth, and he changed quickly. Soon, he stood with his arms crossed, glaring at her and Darius.

"What is the sorcerer doing in Fresthav? Darius, I think you have some explaining to do," Nick chastised him.

"What, were you looking for me? I don't have to explain myself to anyone. What are YOU doing in Fresthav, Nick Chuvash? Does your father know you're here? I think not, as you don't travel with my niece, Mila, or my brother, Aswin."

Nick looked at him with dangerous eyes. He had forgotten that Mila was this man's niece. "Mila is dead, just so you know. I knocked her off the back of my brother, but it was an accident. A damn shame, really."

Darius looked at him. "What? Are you sure? She's dead? You killed my niece?" Gayle squeezed his hand.

"Well, I'm not 100 percent sure. I supposed maybe if she landed in water, or if my brother somehow grabbed her out of the air, she might have survived, but I wouldn't put money on it."

"How dare you!" Darius said, taking a step forward. His staff started glowing, and he had every intention of blasting the Prince with everything he had. Only Gayle's hand on his arm stopped him. She put her lips to his ear. "Do not trust a traitor, Darius. He is filled with lies."

He put his staff down, and just glared at Nick and Sadie with distaste and distrust.

"I've come to talk to Queen Thora. Alone. In private," Nick said, coldly, looking around.

"My mother is unavailable, Nick." A voice from the darkness spoke, and Princess Linnea stepped out, a blond, cold beauty with ice-blue eyes that glared at him. She knew what these two had been planning. After all, her daughter, half night and half ice, would someday marry his son, half sunrise and half summer.

"Well, I guess you'll do then. Can we talk somewhere private?"

"Of course, but my Dragon Keeper and the sorcerer will come with us. I couldn't keep secrets from him anyway, Gayle would tell him," Linnea said disapprovingly. She didn't really like the sorcerer, but he made Gayle happy, so she tolerated him.

"Fine," Nick said glaring at Darius. "I trust you'll hold what I say in confidence."

"Of course," Darius said, rolling his eyes. He was the sorcerer of the Dragon God. He knew pretty much that happened in this world. If the kings didn't blab everything to him when they visited, the Dragon God sometimes sent him visions. He had still been hearing the beats of the drum, but the number of beats had not increased, so he took that as a good sign.

They went upstairs, settling into a cold and drafty parlor. Apparently, Darius and Gayle were the only ones who noticed the cold. Gayle's teeth were chattering, and Darius put his arm around her on the sofa.

"I've put my plan into motion, Linnea," he said with a grin. "By tomorrow night, my father and brother will be dead."

"I see. The plan is moving forward. My mother would be happy to hear this, except she is in a deep sleep, for health reasons. What can I do to help you?"

"I want you to come to Dumara with a force of dragons, not tomorrow, but the day after. Ibis will be there with his men. You two will support me as King of Dumara and help me cement my power. We could even use this time to announce the betrothal of our children."

Linnea considered him. "Are you sure this will work? If we make this move, there is no turning back. You are sure your father and your brother will be dead?"

"Yes, I am sure. I will fly the black flag of mourning off the walls. If you do not see it, you can turn back, but I guarantee it will be there," he said with a smirk.

"Okay then. Gayle, you will come with me," Linnea ordered.

"I'm coming," Darius said. "There is no way I'm letting Gayle go into a potential war zone without me. Are you crazy? This is dangerous." In the back of his head, he was filled with worry. Aswin may be in trouble, and Mila might be dead. He needed to get home and check on them as soon as possible.

"Fine! But you will ride Periwinkle. No drakaina will carry you, sorcerer," Linnea growled.

Gayle smiled at him, glad that he would be coming, with his mighty staff of power. She knew he would look after her.

"I must leave. I need to get back tonight to put the rest of my plan in place." Nick said.

Linnea looked back and forth at the pair. "Fly safe, and I look forward to seeing your victory."

———

Darius was left with Gayle as Linnea went down to the caves. "I should probably restock my bag, if I'm leaving tomorrow," Gayle said.

"Gayle, I've got to get to Dumara tonight. I've got to put a stop to this and check on my brother and niece. This is madness," Darius said. He could feel the balance of power slipping and was afraid the third beat was coming. They inched day by day toward the end, and he felt obligated to stop it.

She stopped and looked at him. "I don't agree with Nick, of course. Murdering your own father and brother is wrong. But if Linnea finds out you actively are trying to stop this, she'll kill me or you or both of us."

"I can go tonight and try to warn them. I just need a dragon."

"I appreciate your thought, but I think it will be noticed if I ask any of the dragons to fly you to Dumara tonight. I love you too much to put you in that danger."

"My niece, she might be dead," Darius begged.

"I know. You'll have to do what you can when we arrive tomorrow. I can't get you a ride to Dumara without raising suspicion. Linnea doesn't like you, and she's a man-eater. Have you seen the way she looks at you?"

"Yeah. I'm not her favorite person. I'll wait, but as soon as we get there, I'm headed for my brother's shop. If we can't reconnect, I'll meet you back at my tower."

"Deal," she said, giving him a quick kiss. "And I'll do what I can on my end. Luckily, Queen Thora is dead asleep, and our connection has been broken since then. She does not know what my traitorous mind is up to."

"That is a bonus," he smiled. "Now, let's go get you ready. Do you think the armory has anything that would fit you?"

"You want me to wear armor?"

"You're potentially going into battle. I think it's a good idea."

"Okay then, let's head there first."

———

Late that night, Nick and Sadie slipped into the caves. He had used the last energy potion to make it home, and he was exhausted. He could sleep for days, but he had a few more things to do before his head found the pillow. Sadie gave him the last astragenica potion, as the Dragon Keeper was long asleep now, and Nick slipped back into human form. He kissed Sadie at the bottom of the stairs.

Sadie whispered in the dark. "I'll just change back into my dragon form and get back to our egg. I'll make sure the girls that are on our side pass the news that the plan is on for tomorrow."

"As soon as you hear the news that my father is dead, stay in your nest. You will be protected, but I don't want to chance anything happening to our egg. I'll come get you when it is safe," he said, squeezing her hand. "The next time I see you, you will be Queen of Dumara."

"And you will be King." A gleam came to her eye.

Nick gave her one last kiss and slipped upstairs. As he passed the dungeon, he smiled. Soon it would be filled with his political enemies, and he took great pleasure in thinking of all the men who would bend to his will or die. The Dragon Keeper was the first one he would start with. Aswin would become his Dragon Keeper or face the consequences.

Nick made his way to his bedroom, finding the bottle of noctum behind a book in his bookshelf. His father had breakfast every morning at 9 o'clock sharp in the conservatory, right after he returned from greeting the sun. If his sons were with him, they joined him.

In the darkness, he slipped down the hall, finding the glass room already set for breakfast tea the next morning. His father was so predictable. The teapot stood dry but pre-filled with leaves.

Carefully, he pulled the cork out of the bottle, being extremely cautious not to spill a drop of the potion on his skin. With an evil grin, he poured the entire bottle into the bottom of the teapot, where tea leaves soaked up the mixture greedily. The servants would be none the wiser; the tea they would serve their King would poison him dead. He would shift the blame to them, give them a quick show trial, and then the throne would be his. His reinforcements from Fresthav and Murdad would secure the city if there was any dissent. It was a perfect plan.

CHAPTER 7

THE THIRD BEAT

R and woke that morning, the last day of his life, and threw open the curtains. Still an hour before dawn, he stretched and yawned. He wondered if Nick had made it back last night.

He grabbed some clothing, brushed his teeth, and drew a brush through his slightly graying hair. He rubbed his beard and then splashed some cold water on his face. He thought about what he had to do today. He would greet the sun, have breakfast, and then a meeting later in the morning with the head of the treasury and his head counsel. After lunch, he would meet with the Captain of the Amber May, a very early trading ship that had just arrived from Norda. She had been trying to get ahead of the rush, and the captain was meeting with him to secure a valuable shipment of iron.

Ready to start his day, he stepped into the hall. Alex and Nick were waiting for him, standing far apart and not talking. The tension in the hallway was thick. Nick must have gotten in late last night because he looked like he hadn't really slept. His eyes were bloodshot, and his clothes were rumpled.

Rand tilted his head, wondering what Nick had been up to.

"Son, I would ask you where you were yesterday, but we can talk about it after we greet the sun. I'm sure you will have a good story for me."

"Of course, Father. Sorry for not keeping you updated. I've been making some deals, but I didn't want to tell you before they were cemented. We can discuss over breakfast," Nick said, quickly, with a small smile on his face.

"Let's go then. The sun sleeps and it's up to us to nudge him forward," Rand said with a grin. When Cassandra was still alive, this was their favorite part of the day. It wasn't the same without her, but he liked it best when he had his family and clan around him. There was something so invigorating about flying together, wing tip to wing tip, and feeling the sun's power.

They hurried downstairs, Alex and Nick still not talking. He would have to figure out a way to get these boys to see eye to eye. Their constant bickering would be the death of him.

A handful of dragons had joined them at the entrance, and soon, they were all airborne, heading due east. A very thin sliver of sun peeked over the horizon, and as they roared, it made an appearance. Soon, their large shimmering bodies of red, gold, and orange were lit with the rays of the sun, and they roared with joy.

———

Nick smoothly lied to his father that morning. It didn't really matter what he said, because his father would believe anything that came out of his mouth. Rand trusted him, which was his first mistake. They made it back to the caves in just under an hour, and as Nick came in for a landing, he felt a little anxious. What if his plan didn't go as he had envisioned?

Aswin was busy this morning, but quickly changed all three of them. As soon as they were dressed, their father turned to them. "You have time for breakfast, boys? I want to talk to Nick about what he did yesterday."

"Of course, Father," Nick said brightly. Alex was scowling at him, his arms crossed.

"I don't know if I care," Alex said angrily, his eyes hooded.

"Are you still mad about Mila? I told you it was an accident. I didn't even know you were following me. How was I supposed to know?" Nick said, feigning sorrow.

"She's not dead, you know. I managed to grab her," Alex said, as he joined his father, moving up the stairs. Aswin hadn't said a word to any of them this morning, and Alex had caught his scowl at Nick, so he knew that the Dragon Keeper had heard the story.

"Oh," Nick said, and then he retorted brightly, "That's good. I was feeling a little guilty. I'm glad you grabbed her, of course."

They entered the conservatory. The morning sun was shining through the glass panes, and the plants were bright green and lush. They sat at the table, and Rand considered the bright day. "It's been a warm spring. I'm glad the winter is over."

"Me, too. Fresthav was still cold yesterday," Nick noted, watching the servants bring in breakfast scones and muffins.

"Tell me what you have been up to," Rand said, grabbing a muffin off the tray.

Alex turned red and glared at Nick. "Yes, brother. When I saw you, you were headed for Murdad. Did you visit Murdad and Fresthav both in one day?"

Nick grabbed a muffin and sat it on his plate. "Where is the tea?" he asked anxiously, looking around. He hoped no one had discovered the leaves were already wet and had thrown them out. That would be disastrous.

"One minute, sir, we are just waiting on the hot water to be brought from the kitchen," the servant said, placing a bowl of berries in the center of the table.

"Well, while we wait, I'll guess I'll start. I visited both kingdoms yesterday. I'm sorry I didn't tell you, Father. But I had my reasons," Nick said, desperately trying to buy time.

"Yes, Nick, tell us your reasons," Alex said, rolling his eyes.

A servant came in with a steaming kettle of water. He poured it into the china teapot. "Just let that steep a few minutes."

"Could I have some fruit juice? I'm going to sleep after this, and tea will keep me up. I got in late last night," Nick asked. He had thought this all out before. It would give him a legitimate reason to have escaped the poison.

"Of course, sir. I'll bring you some cloudberry juice from the kitchen. Fresh pressed just this morning." The servant hurried off.

"So, as I was saying, I had my reasons. I've become friendly with Kai Monserrat, and I didn't think you would approve."

"I don't really, Nick. When would you have the opportunity to become friendly with Kai?" his father asked, taking a bite of his muffin.

"The same way I met Sadie, hunting on the northern border. It's amazing how much you can accomplish if you just talk to people instead of chasing them away. They want what we want, peace."

"Well, that's interesting. The last time I checked, it was them who constantly caused problems by coming into our territory to hunt."

"It's all a misunderstanding. They come into our territory to hunt, but it's because they must. Their herds are thin, and they risk overhunting."

"So, they come into our territory, and risk the health of our herds? That makes little sense, Nick." Rand looked at him with a raised eyebrow. He picked up the teapot and poured himself a cup.

He put the teapot down, and Alex picked it back up, pouring himself a full cup.

"Well, I've worked out a deal with them. They stay just north of the sorcerer's tower, in the woods and field just south of the Great Divide, and we agree not to attack them. This will reduce tension."

"This is not a solution, Nick. You are missing the point." Rand added cream and sugar to his tea, stirring with a teaspoon. Alex was paused, with his teacup halfway to his mouth, but his mouth was hanging open, looking at his brother in disbelief.

"But I think it is a solution," Nick said, staring at the cup in his father's hand. He picked up his fruit juice that had just arrived. The servant was waiting off to the right, in case anyone needed anything else. He took a drink. The sharp tang of the cloudberries hit his tongue, and he gulped the entire glass down. He sat it down carefully and then looked back at his father.

Rand sighed, and then took a deep drink of his tea, draining half of the cup in one drink.

Alex shook his head and blew on his tea. It was hot, and because he didn't take cream, it had not cooled down. He took a sip to taste the heat, and it burned his mouth.

He blew on it again and paused as he brought the rim of the glass to his lips. It tasted oily and wrong. Suddenly, he felt strange. His head felt light, and the world spun. He grabbed the edge of the table and looked at Nick in alarm.

Next to him, the cup slipped out of his father's hands, spilling the remaining tea everywhere. Rand fell out of his chair, onto the floor, where he convulsed, his eyes rolling back in his head.

Alex watched all this in horror and saw an evil smile on his brother's face. The servant rushed to Rand, and he heard screaming. That was the last thing he remembered before the world went black, and the visions began.

———

In Murdad, twenty dragons swirled out of the caves just after dawn. On their backs were armored soldiers carrying polearms. They headed straight south, led by the roars of Ibis and Kai, urging them on.

General Atam was at Ibis's side, riding Grenadier. He blew a horn, and the dragons moved into a point formation. The ground rolled under them, and farmers heard the sound of trumpets above and rushed out to look up. In one glance, they knew war had come to the Kingdom of Dumara, and they trembled with fear. The day seemed to dim, as the force of the dark energy bursts covered the sky.

———

To the west, Linnea gathered her troops, leaving only a handful of dragons at the castle to guard her mother. "Let nothing happen to her. If she wakes up, which I doubt, let her know that war has finally come. We ride to Dumara!"

Gayle was on her back, and she threw a glance at Darius, who looked worried. He was astride Periwinkle, holding on tightly. He had never really ridden a dragon, and it was harder than he had expected. Maybe it was because Periwinkle hated him. When told the sorcerer would ride him, he growled, "You had better not pull my mane, or I'll throw you off, and you will be crushed from the fall."

So, Darius was afraid to even touch his mane, and Periwinkle wasn't being kind, moving suddenly, as if he wanted the sorcerer off his back.

"Periwinkle, if anything happens to Darius, you know, by accident, I'm holding you personally responsible. You had better make sure nothing happens to him!" Gayle ordered, authority filling her voice.

"Yes, ma'am," Periwinkle said, lowering his head. After that, it was much easier to keep his seat, and Darius held on to the dragon's mane with one hand, clasping his staff in the other.

The dragons flew over the thawed plains of Fresthav, green buds just erupting from the cold ground, working up to their one week of flowering, until they retreated again when the ice dragons covered the world with snow.

The dragons roared, and the ice blew out of their mouths, covering the world with a layer of frost as they went by.

The farmers below felt the frost and heard the roaring. They ran outside and saw the group of the winter dragons fly by. They shivered as their wives threw another log on the fire, and they knew war had come.

———

BOOM BOOM BOOM. Three drumbeats sounded. Mila, in a dead sleep, was catapulted out of her dreams by the sound. She sat up straight in bed, her heart thumping. Something was wrong.

She reached out with her mind to Alex, but there was nothing. Only silence. In a panic, she fumbled around in the dark, her ribs and body still aching. She threw open the curtains and found it was about an hour after dawn. Her father must have let her sleep. She hurried to dress, feeling frantic. She must get to the castle.

Sam was sweeping the store when she ran downstairs. "Sam! Something is wrong. Did you hear the drums?"

"No, what drums, Mila?" he asked with concern. "Are you okay?"

"No, I'm not. I've got to get to the castle. Something is wrong, terribly wrong."

"I found that bag for you this morning. I stocked it for you. And I left some pain powder out for you. I thought you might need it."

"Thank you so much, Sam!" she said, giving him a quick hug.

He looked surprised and returned her hug awkwardly. "No problem."

"Listen, keep the shop closed. I feel like something is dreadfully wrong. If everything is fine, I'll be back, and we can reopen. But I don't feel Alex. It's like he's gone from my mind. Not even a whisper." She frantically grabbed her cloak from the hook by the door.

"Has that ever happened before?" he said, his eyes going wide.

"No, never," she yelled as she hurried out the door.

———

Down in the caves, Aswin had done his morning duties, surprised that Nick made an appearance to greet the sun, surprised that he was even here this morning. He guessed they had gotten back late last night, and Sadie had changed him. He peeked into Nick's cave, and Sadie was sleeping soundly, wrapped up around her egg.

He was in Dahlia's cave now, checking on her and the egg. He had sensed that she had been sad lately and came to offer her some herbs. "You need to get out, Dahlia. It's not healthy for you to stay here in your nest day after day, with no sunlight. Sunrise dragons need the sun."

"Dragon Keeper, I cannot leave my egg. I fear Sadie or one of her minions will crush it. I could leave it with my friends, but even then, I fear betrayal," she said sadly.

"I understand, but you have to get out. Maybe Mila and I could watch it for you. No one would dare smash your egg if one of us were here," he offered.

She looked at him, moving her face so that her yellow eyes stared into his. "Thank you, Dragon Keeper. I may take you up on that offer."

Just then, Aswin felt a wrenching pain in his forehead. BOOM BOOM BOOM! He heard, and it rang through his ears.

"What was that?" Dahlia's voice rose in alarm.

Aswin stumbled against her rock nest. The pain was unbearable. He gasped, tears rolling down his face.

"Dragon Keeper, are you okay? What happened?"

He took a deep breath as the initial pain receded. He reached out to Rand, but there was nothing. Only a deep, profound silence. "It's gone. My connection is gone," he whispered, looking at Dahlia in horror.

"Connection? You speak in riddles, Aswin."

"Something is horribly wrong, Dahlia. I must go. Protect your egg at all costs!" He grabbed his bag, stumbling slightly. His balance was wrong, and the world spun. He made it to the long hallway that led to the stairs. All around him, he heard muttering. The dragons had heard the booms, and they were all scared.

He put his foot on the first step, looking up at the spiral stairs which lead into the darkness. He didn't know how he was going to do this. He felt terrible. But he took it a stair at a time, clutching the wall for support.

———

Upstairs, the castle was in an uproar. Nick made a show of trying to revive his father and brother. They were both lying on the floor of the conservatory, the tea glasses broken on the floor in shards around their bodies.

Servants stood around, not knowing what to do. Occasionally, someone would feel for a pulse, and then start crying when they couldn't find one.

Nick leapt into motion, ordering his Dragon Keepers to be found, and to lock the castle gates.

"There has been a crime committed here today. My father and brother have been poisoned by a traitor! We must find the assassin!"

The head of his castle guards appeared. This was Nick's man. "Start an investigation, secure the walls. No one must leave or enter. We will find who did this, and they will pay for their crimes."

A servant approached him, the same servant who had served the tea. "Your Majesty, I promise you, I had nothing to do with this. I would never hurt the King or your brother!"

"A likely story. Seize this man. We will question him later."

"Sir, what should we do with the bodies?" another servant asked, tears dripping down his face.

"Cover them for now. I need Aswin. Find him. He should be in the caves," Nick said, looking at the bodies. His father's bright blue eyes were open and staring at the ceiling. Alex's were closed, and he was laying on his side, with his hand reaching for his father.

The King's Counsel and the Head of the Treasury both appeared, looking concerned. They had been in the castle for the meeting with King Rand. They both spotted the bodies on the floor and gasped.

"There has been a murder," Nick said. "I have put the full efforts of the castle guards into motion."

"So, you are the King? This is a tragedy, but I will serve you," the King's Counsel said with a bow.

"And I will serve you also," the Treasurer said, bowing his head. "May the Dragon God have mercy on their souls."

"The meeting is canceled, obviously. Go to your homes, I will call upon you when needed," Nick said, turning and walking from the room.

His mind whirled. He had to secure the city, and the dragons must be subdued. He knew he would have problems in both places, but he had men on the inside already taking action.

A soldier rushed by. "Stop!" Nick ordered. "Go to the walls and run the black mourning banner. Do it immediately."

The man turned, "It's true then, the King is dead?" he asked in horror.

"It is true, and my brother is also gone," Nick said, letting a touch of sadness come to his voice. He turned and made straight for the throne room. He would run things from there, and by the end of the day, his rule would be secure.

CHAPTER 8

THE APPROACHING STORM

S am was in the workshop, mixing up the daily batch of astragenica, when he heard the banging on the front door. Muttering to himself, he made his way to the front. Through the glass, he could see soldiers out on the street.

He opened the door to a soldier, with his fist upraised. "The King is dead. The Crown Prince is dead. Stores are to remain closed until further notice. Lock up, we're expecting trouble," the soldier said bluntly, turning to leave.

"What kind of trouble?" Sam said, worry crossing his face. This was bad, and probably why Mila had left so quickly this morning. He glanced up at the castle. She was up there somewhere.

"Looting perhaps. We don't know. King Nick is moving to secure the city," the soldier said, hurtling down the stairs.

Across the street, he could see his father-in-law, Franklin Wright, talking with a soldier. He turned his sign to closed and shut the door.

"Hades," Sam said, glancing around. He didn't know what to do, besides follow orders. If looting started, it's not like he could do much, besides protect the store with a broomstick. Maybe he could find something in the basement.

But first, he hurried across the street, letting himself into the tailor's shop with his key, and then relocking the door behind him.

Kiera rushed forward; her eyes were wet with tears. "You heard the news? The King and Crown Prince are dead? How can this be?"

Sam hugged his wife. She was pregnant with their first child, and already showing. Franklin came up to the front, worry on his face. "I don't know what's going on. Mila and Aswin are both gone. The only thing we can do is wait and hope the criminals don't use this power shift to their advantage."

"I've got weapons," Franklin said, opening a closet where they kept cleaning supplies. He pulled out an old sword, covered with streamers and ribbons, and a thick bat, which he handed to his wife, Judith.

"What about me, Father? I need a weapon," Kiera said, looking back and forth between her parents.

"You all should come across the street with me. If worse comes to worst, we can hide in the sewers. Aswin has a secret passage," he said.

"I'll keep that in mind, but I'm staying here. I've spent my life building this place, and I'll let someone loot it over my dead body. Kiera, you go with Sam," her father ordered, pointing to the door.

"Okay, Father, you two stay safe, and don't go playing hero. If someone wants old bolts of fabric, just let them take it," she admonished, moving to the front with her husband, but knowing her father wouldn't let anyone mess with his livelihood. Luckily, he had a safe upstairs in his closet, where he kept most of their fortune. She knew that no matter what, he would never give anyone the combination of that safe, which was her birthday, 0106.

Sam led her across the street. Everything seemed quiet, except he could hear a roar from the south. With a sinking heart, he knew it was coming from the docks, the seediest part of the city. He doubted things would stay peaceful. The criminal underworld would jump at the chance to disrupt things if they could. He glanced to the west and noticed rain clouds forming. They were dark and ominous. He felt the tension around him waiting to erupt, and he hurried inside the shop, Kiera following close behind. He slammed the door and locked it, looking around. "We might need some way to barricade this door if the time comes. Help me clear off this display of potions. If we need to, we can move it in front of the door."

Kiera nodded and moved the bottles and tins to the counter. She was scared, and if she threw her mind into this task, she could push that fear down.

———

Mila had hurried up to the castle gates. Everything was eerily quiet. As she approached the castle, she noticed something different. A company of soldiers was gathering near the gates, and a commander was shouting out orders. She stopped in her tracks to listen.

"Men! The King is dead, along with the Crown Prince. We move to secure the city. I want squadron A to go to the Main Street and order the shops all closed. Squadron B will go to the town square, shoo all the citizens away, and tell the stalls they must close. Then, once that is done, both A and B squads will patrol the residential neighborhoods. Watch for any signs of unrest.

"Squadron C will head straight for the docks. This is where we expect trouble. Warn the ship captains at dock and secure the slums. Use deadly force if necessary."

Mila's knees threatened to buckle under her. The King and Alex, dead? It couldn't be. It was impossible. But in her heart, she knew it was true. She choked back a cry and steeled herself. She had to see for herself.

As the squadrons and their leaders marched out of the gates, she approached the man on duty hesitantly.

"Sir, I am Mila Fletcher, Dragon Keeper. It is imperative I see the King imminently."

"Of course, we have orders to find you. You've made our job

easy," he snapped his fingers, and a soldier stepped forward. "Take Mila to King Nick. He wants to see her."

Her heart fell. Instantly, she knew Nick was behind this all. He had tried to kill her yesterday, after all.

She was even more alarmed when the soldier grabbed her arm roughly, pulling her along. She tried to pull away from him. "Stop, you're hurting me. I'll come with you."

He took his hand off her, glaring at her the entire time. She adjusted her bag, and followed, wondering where her father was, and if he felt the same emptiness in his head that she did.

———

Aswin made it up the stairs, gasping and holding his head. He practically fell out of the door into the main hallway. He squinted as the light blinded him, and another searing bolt of pain ripped through his head.

A guard standing at the door to the stairway gasped. "Mr. Fletcher, are you okay?" he worried, helping him rise.

"I've had better days. Where is the King? I need to see him immediately," Aswin demanded.

"Sir, I'm sorry to tell you, but King Rand is dead, and the Crown Prince with him. Treachery is afoot. King Nick has ordered that we find you and bring you to him."

"King Nick, you don't say?" Aswin said, frowning. He knew where the treachery lay. He would not help the man who killed his friend.

He was led to the throne room, stumbling once or twice. This must be the aftereffect of his mind connection being broken. He was filled with sadness.

As they entered the throne room, he saw Nick sitting on his father's throne, looking down at him coldly. He wasn't really surprised to see Mila already there, tears streaming down her face.

"Ahh, just in time. I was just telling Mila here about the unfortunate death this morning of my father and brother. It looks like poisoning. I'm on the hunt and will get to the bottom of this."

Mila remained quiet, but Aswin could sense the fury rising in her. He knew his daughter, and normally, she was quiet and reserved, but occasionally, when her temper was up, she would release her built up fury, and it would explode like a supernova. He shook his head at her, realizing they both were in very dangerous territory.

"I trust that both of my Dragon Keepers will continue to serve me faithfully," Nick said, a cold hard smile on his face.

Aswin bowed his head, not trusting himself to speak.

"Very well then. You may return to your duties."

"I need to see the bodies," Aswin found his voice. "They need to be properly prepared, according to the rituals of the Dragon God. And they will be moved to the crypts, as is the custom of Kings."

"But they died in their human forms, not their dragon forms," Nick said, confused.

"It doesn't happen often, but they still need to be interred in the crypts. It is only right that Rand and Alex should rest with their ancestors."

"Fine. They are still in the conservatory. I was going to have the priests come later, and transport them to the cathedral for the funerals, but I suppose we can play the old game we played with mother, and have the caskets filled with stones," Nick said dismissively. "Although I would have loved a good open casket, so the people could grieve."

"Thank you, Your Majesty," Aswin said, bowing his head. "Mila and I will take care of this important ritual for you. You have many pressing matters to take care of today. I worry the city will erupt in violence. I'm concerned that the clan won't accept you."

"I am the King. Why would they not accept me? Besides, I already have that taken care of. I am expecting some guests later today. Stay out of their way if you know what's good for you," Nick threatened.

"Guests?" Aswin asked, rising an eyebrow. "Anyone I know?"

"Guards, take them to the bodies and provide whatever assistance they need." Nick waved them away without answering Aswin's question, and two guards appeared.

Mila and Aswin left the throne room with the guards, who led them upstairs, toward the conservatory.

"Father, what was that all about? You aren't going to serve him, are you? I'm certainly not going to," she whispered.

"Shhh, Mila. We need to tread carefully. No, I'm not going to, but we need to see for ourselves what he has done," Aswin said. The guards noticed them whispering and frowned at them.

They were led into the room, and Mila cried out as she saw the two figures covered with sheets. She pulled back the first one, revealing the slack face of Rand.

Aswin rushed forward, finding himself suddenly blinded by grief. His old friend, dead before him, was too much to bear. His head still pounded as he touched him, feeling for his pulse and confirming he was dead. He shook his head sadly and pushed back a sob.

Mila had moved to the second body, and with a shaking hand, pulled down the sheet. She knew what she would see, but the sight of Alex, lying prone on his side, his hand outstretched, felt like a stab in the heart. She sat back in disbelief. Just yesterday, they had flown together. He had saved her, grabbing her out of the sky, and now he lay lifeless before her.

Aswin turned to the guards. "We are going to need two stretchers and at least two more men. We need to take them to the crypts below."

"Yes sir, we will be back shortly," they said and hurried off.

Mila's tears rolled down her face, and she reached out a hand to touch him. She placed her hand on his chest to roll him onto his back. Suddenly, she pulled her hand away. "Father, I don't think he is dead. He's warm!"

Aswin scrambled to his side. He felt for a pulse, his fingers probing. Finally, he found it. It was faint, so faint, but it was there, and his body was warm. "He's alive, but barely so. Look in your bag, quickly, before the guards come back. You are looking for capsicum. Slip some under his tongue. Quickly now!"

Mila hurried, scrambling as she threw open her bag. Everything was neatly labeled inside, bless Sam. She quickly found the capsicum power, opening the packet with shaking fingers. She opened Alex's mouth, probing with her finger, and poured the powder under his tongue.

Meanwhile, her father was looking over the scene. He saw the broken teacups, and the teapot, still filled with lukewarm tea sitting on the table. He picked it up and sniffed it. There was an oily black sheen on top of the water. "Noctum, I guarantee it. Alex must have only taken a sip."

Aswin poured the tea onto a plant in the back of the room. It was dangerous to leave this here in the open. If anyone even touched it, they would probably have terrible side effects. He threw the teapot on the floor, smashing it into pieces. "Oops," he said, frowning.

His mind, although still in pain, was spinning. He looked over at Mila. It made sense she wasn't in the same pain as him. "You don't feel anything? Any connection at all?"

"No, it's like he's not here."

"But you aren't feeling any pain?"

"No, do you feel pain?"

"Yes, a splitting headache. I can barely walk straight. My connection, after all these years, has been broken. Mila, we've got to act fast. This is treason by Nick. If he finds out Alex is still alive, I have a feeling he will make sure he's dead. Nick wanted the throne, and now he's got it."

"What can we do?"

"Alex got a strong dose. Nearly lethal. My brother would tell you that noctom is dangerous. He must have made it. He's the only one who holds the secret. It will give a person powerful visions, but any more than a few drops will kill. He might still die, his pulse is so weak, the poison is still in his system."

"So, we wait?" Mila said, concern coming over her face.

"Yes, but we don't have the time. He's going to need care; I think he got a huge dose. We need to get him out of Dumara. It's too dangerous for him here. But we have the advantage. Nick believes he is dead," Aswin said, pacing frantically as his mind raced.

"And if Alex is dead, then obviously he isn't a problem to be worried about," Mila said, feeling again for a pulse. She found it now, faint under her fingers.

"Yes, and he needs to remain dead, for now. Hurry, hide him," Aswin ordered. Mila kissed Alex's cheek and then covered him again with the sheet.

The guards reappeared with two stretchers. Stopping his frantic pacing, Aswin directed them to move the bodies to the stretchers. He himself lifted Alex's chest, letting the guard take the feet. He wanted no chance that anyone but Mila and himself knew Alex was still alive.

———

Down on the docks, the gangs gathered. "The King is dead! Now is our time to take what is ours!" they shouted, the mob swelling.

"Prince Nick is a dirty usurper! Let's give the throne to the people!" others shouted.

The mob moved in force, carrying torches, knives, swords, hoes, bricks. They were full of hatred. They wanted to line their pockets in this period of unrest, guessing the new King would be grief stricken and unprepared to lead. There was no better time for a little redistribution of wealth.

The mass moved toward the north, toward the merchant district, encountering no one. It seemed like the streets were still empty, every door and window locked and shuttered.

"Let's head to the merchant distinct. The rich can open their doors for us. They won't be hurting if we take a few things," the ringleader chuckled, pointing up Grand Avenue. The way was clear. The soldiers hadn't arrived yet, and the mob moved as one, chanting all the way, growing and swelling as people joined them. By the time the soldiers arrived, the mob outnumbered them three to one. There was a quick bloody skirmish, and then the squad of soldiers from the castle retreated. They now were in dangerous territory.

———

The dragons in the cave were filled with fear as the news percolated that the King and his son were dead. The dragons gathered in the main area as wild rumors spread. Some said the King and both his sons were dead, others said that it was only the King, while others accused Nick outright of murder.

Torrid was the one leading the criticism. "We all know Nick has been sowing seeds of malcontent among us. He sneaks off at all hours. I wouldn't put it past him to do something like this. We all know he wants the throne for himself."

Sumac, leader of the little pack of outcasts that always surrounded Nick, now had gathered the ones loyal to the new King. "Watch what you say, Torrid, or you may be labeled a traitor."

"I am not a traitor, but we will not be ruled by a man who may have killed his own father! Rand was a close friend of mine. I want answers!" Torrid roared, and mumbles of consent arose from behind him.

"Nick will have answers. You need to settle down, Torrid. Wait until we know more," Sumac said menacingly.

"Oh, you think I fear you? Ha ha ha," Torrid sneered, and his friends moved forward.

Sumac sensed he was over his head right now. He did not take the bait, but he didn't back down either. "Just wait a few hours. We will find out more," he said, pleading with desperation. He had to stall; both Murdad and Fresthav were on their way, and that is when the real fighting would start. The clan would submit, or they would die.

———

Aswin and Mila arrived down in the caves, with the guards carrying the stretchers with the covered bodies. As they moved through the hallways, the dragons saw them. "It's true then, King Rand is dead. And Alex with him?"

Aswin nodded, not revealing the secret. He didn't know who was an enemy, and who was a friend. They moved to the main hall, where Torrid and his group of warriors, and Sumac, with his group of misfits, were still arguing.

Audible gasps were heard as the dragons saw the covered bodies. "It's true! The King is dead." Dragons lowered themselves to the ground, their heads bowed in respect. They stopped in front of Torrid and Sumac.

"It is true. I'm sorry you are the last to know. King Rand and Alex were poisoned this morning at breakfast. It appears someone laced their tea. Prince Nick survived somehow. I'll let you make your own deductions," Aswin said, as the guards lowered the stretchers.

Aswin pulled back the sheet that covered Rand, and it was clear to all that the King was dead, his eyes looking up, unseeing. Sobs were heard.

"Where is Dahlia? I must tell her that her mate is gone," Aswin said, looking around.

"She will not leave her egg," Torrid said. "I will go tell her."

"Mila and I will take the body to her, so that she can say her goodbyes."

"I want to go with you. My daughter will be upset," Torrid insisted.

"Very well, we will stop there before we go on to the crypts," Aswin said, motioning to the guards to pick up the bodies.

They moved down the hallway, a sad sight indeed, and then the panicked whispers started.

———

The dragons were still, honoring the dead, but anger was festering. They all had heard Aswin's words and had concluded that Nick had killed his father and brother. All eyes turned to Sumac. "You will all go back to your nests," the dragon demanded, and his misfits moved forward.

Lacking Torrid to lead them, no one spoke.

"Go back to your nests! I demand it!" Sumac said, his voice cracking.

"Why don't you make us, Sumac?" a voice from the rear said, and Chain, a friend of Torrid's, stepped forward. "I think you're outnumbered. We want to remain here; we have much to talk about."

"You'll be sorry," Sumac squeaked and backed down.

"I thought so," Chain said. "Now, let's talk about what we are going to do. None of us want Nick as King."

———

Aswin and Mila entered Dahlia's nest quietly. She had her back turned to them, and she was staring at the wall. "Dahlia. We've come."

"Is it true," she whispered. "Alex is dead? My dragonling will never know his father?"

Mila looked at the guards who were carrying the stretcher. They looked uncomfortable and out of place. "If you could step out for a moment, we need privacy."

"Ahh, sure," one man said, leaving the bodies and stepping out into the hallway.

Dahlia was looking at the stretchers. Tears started leaking from her eyes. "He's dead."

"My daughter. I'm sorry. It's true. My grief is with you, as it is with the entire clan," Torrid said, moving forward to his daughter.

"Dahlia, listen to me," Mila said, opening her arms to the dragon. She climbed into the nest and got close to Dahlia's head.

93

Dahlia lowered her head, grief in her eyes. "He's not dead, Dahlia. But he's near death," Mila whispered.

Torrid overheard her whisper and startled. He turned to look at the stretchers behind him.

"Can you save him, Dragon Keeper?" Dahlia cried, trying to keep her voice low.

"I think so. But we've got to get him out of here. If Nick finds out he's still alive, well, he'll make sure he's dead."

"My egg! Nick will come for my egg!" Dahlia fretted.

They all looked at Dahlia's egg, shining gold and red in the torchlight.

"We can smuggle it away, Dahlia. We are going to smuggle Alex out of the caves. As soon as we can, we can take the egg with him."

"Take it then, and godspeed," Dahlia said,."Let me look at my husband. Who knows if I will see him alive again?"

Aswin pulled the sheet down and checked his pulse again. "His pulse is stronger, the capsicum you gave him earlier must be working. Here, give me the egg, we will put it between his legs, and he will keep the egg warm."

"How does he still live, Aswin? He looks dead," Torrid said, his voice full of uncertainty.

Dahlia looked down on the face of her husband and choked back a sob. He looked like he was sleeping. His blue eyes closed; his mouth slightly parted. Mila picked up the fragile egg and placed it gently between Alex's legs, and then covered them both with the sheet. You could not tell the egg was there.

"Hurry, Dragon Keeper. Please, save my family," Dahlia said.

"We will go to the crypts. No one will think to look there."

"It is forbidden to the living, so that is a good hiding place," Torrid said.

"Torrid, I need you to do something very important. I need you to fly to Terrek and warn King Cleon. I fear Nick and Sadie will turn their attention to him soon. He needs to know what treachery has occurred. They are our allies, and Cleon will be most vexed to hear his friend is dead," Aswin said.

"I will fly immediately. Are you going to smuggle Alex to Terrek?" Torrid asked.

"No, I have a better idea. He will be beyond the reach of any dragon," Aswin said.

"Let us go, it is deep in the mountain, and it will take us some time to get there. Guards!" Aswin shouted, and the four men peeked back in.

"We are ready. Mila and I will lead the way with torches," Aswin said. The guards picked up the stretchers and they started forward.

Torrid hurried to the entrance. Without saying a word, he leapt out of the air. The assembled dragons looked after him, wondering what was going on.

Torrid turned to the east, startled by a mass of purple dragons appearing on the horizon. Nightfall dragons! He knew at that moment that all was lost, and that his clan was all but destroyed. He flew as quickly as possible eastward, pumping his huge wings as fast as he could. Time was of the essence.

———

The nightfall dragons arrived first, with trumpets blowing. Ibis and Kai led the way. They saw the ramparts of the city below them, with the black flag flying.

"He did it, by God. I didn't think he would pull it off," Doyle said with glee as they flew over the city.

They dropped down to the town square, and the few people shopping scrambled, and ran, throwing their shopping on the ground in their haste to escape. The soldiers climbed off and gathered. "Men! We will move to the east and make sure the path to the castle is guarded."

"Are you ready, Doyle? We are going in, prepare for a fight!" Ibis chuckled.

"Ready for a good fight. It's been a while, friend," Doyle said, raising his fist into the air and whooping. "I feel young today!"

The nightfall dragons took off again and reached the opening of the caves in a blink of an eye. Ibis flared his wings as they neared the entrance to the dragon caves.

The sunrise dragons were completely unprepared, and as the purple nightfall dragons filled their main hall, they roared with alarm, claws out, and they fought to hold them back.

———

Darius and Gayle were on the backs of their dragons, flying side by side. Darius had found a leather breastplate for Gayle and outfitted her with a helmet. She looked fierce, like a shield maiden of old. She grinned at Darius and struck a pose.

Linnea had been impatient to go. They had flown all morning, until the city of Dumara appeared below, the black flag flying.

"He's done it. That lying traitor actually killed his father. I can't believe it," Darius said, fear catching in his throat.

Gayle listened for a moment, and then turned to Darius. "We are going straight to the caves."

"I need to go to my brother's shop. I need to see if everything is okay," Darius insisted.

Gayle reached for her medallion on her throat. She spoke to Periwinkle. "You need to land in the town square to let Darius dismount, then join us in the caves up above."

"I am not your servant. I am not a stagecoach," Periwinkle growled, malice dripping from his voice.

"Do as my Dragon Keeper commands. Besides, we don't want him in the way," Linnea said as she flew.

"Fine!" Periwinkle roared.

Gayle turned to Darius. "He will drop you off, but he's not happy about it."

Darius said, "Remember, if we can't find each other, meet me at my tower. Be safe!"

"I will! You keep safe also!" Gayle said, waving as they turned toward the caves.

Darius could tell Periwinkle was angry from the way he flew. His shoulders were tense, and he was focused solely on the landing. He landed hard, and Darius was thrown off his back. His staff went flying, and he rolled to a stop. Before he could even get up, Periwinkle was back in the sky, headed straight for the caves.

Darius stood up, brushing himself off. He was bruised and battered from the rough landing. He picked up his staff with a groan and looked around. He was in the town square, but he was the only living soul. The place was quiet, like a ghost town. He looked around and saw someone peeking at him from an upstairs window, but when he looked again, they were gone. People were scared. He turned toward the street that led to his brother's shop and heard shouting from the distance. It seemed to come from the south.

He was hobbling; he had hit his knee hard, and it was tender and swelling up. He used his staff as a cane, trying to walk as fast as he could. He came to the intersection of Grand Avenue and South Street. As he neared the corner, he could hear shouting. He turned his head to the left and saw a huge mob waving weapons and torches in the air. He heard the sound of smashing glass, and a roar went up in the mob.

As fast as he could, he crossed the street and continued up Grand. Things were getting dangerous.

Store after store he passed was closed. He stopped for a moment, realizing that he was in front of the paper maker's shop. Here was where Leah had lived with her family. The business had been sold years ago, but it still shocked him. The memories threatened to overwhelm him. How could he have been so stupid?

He shook his head and continued, coming to his brother's shop soon enough. The sign on the door read CLOSED, and he looked inside. It was dark.

He tried to open the door, but it was locked. He banged on the door, but here was no answer.

Finally, having no other option, he lowered his staff. "APERTA CINNE!" he demanded, the blue power oozing out of the stone on the top of his staff and into the lock. The lock opened with a click, and he stepped inside. His eyes took a moment to adjust to the light, and as they did, he saw Sam, the shopkeeper, looking at him dangerously. He was holding a broom over his head.

"Stop! I'm Darius Fletcher! Don't you remember me?" he shouted, raising his staff into the air.

"Of course. Sorry, I thought you were a looter. I've got my wife here," Sam said, and a scared-looking young woman stepped out from behind him.

"There are riots coming. They are just down a few blocks. I suspect when they reach Grand, they will head straight down this way," Darius warned.

"Hades," Sam said, moving back to the door. He closed it and locked it again. "I guess it's time to barricade the door."

"Where is my brother? Where is Mila? Is she okay?" Darius asked frantically.

"They both went up to the castle. Mila is okay. She was hurt yesterday, and she arrived back last night a little beat up. You've heard the news; the King and Alex were poisoned?"

"Poisoned?" Darius said, his heart sinking. He wished he had never made that batch of noctum for Ibis. If he would have known that was the intention, he wouldn't have made it. "Noctum, I bet. The King is dead, and that odorous boil Nick has stolen the throne. He has conspired with Queen Thora and King Monserrat. The dragons are in the caves now, taking it over."

"The Dragon Keepers are in danger," Sam said, looking out the window in the castle's direction.

"Maybe, but Nick needs them. He knows that. I doubt he will hurt them."

Just then, shouts were heard from down the street. "I think they are coming," Sam said, his eyes going wide. "Help me with this shelf. We are going to barricade the door."

CHAPTER 9

HALLS OF THE DEAD

The sad group bore the bodies down into the heart of the mountain, taking the old, nearly forgotten paths deeper and deeper into the darkness. Here, no dragon tread, unless they were being drug by their families to their last resting place. The floor was worn smooth from the huge hulks of dragons scraping against the ground, and the hall was twice as wide as normal, as it took four dragons to move the corpse of a deceased one.

The pair of stretchers were easily carried. Aswin shivered as he reached the first layer of the catacombs, and not just because they were cold. Family crypts lined the hallway, and each crypt was essentially a large hole in the floor. Bodies of the dead were placed in the hole to spend eternity surrounded by the bones of their ancestors. Once they were decomposed, the next body would be placed on top. It was quite the efficient system.

Aswin had not been down in quite some time. Occasionally, they needed dragon bone or teeth as ingredients for the workshop, and Aswin visited the oldest parts of the crypt and took what he needed from the crypt of miscreants, the bodies of those deemed not worthy of the family crypt. Those that were shunned and outcast because of crimes such as murder or rape, which weren't common, but happened from time to time. Aswin hoped Nick ended up there someday, but he wouldn't take any bets.

They neared the series of Chuvash crypts. There were four of them, two of them filled to the brim with the bones of Chuvash Kings. The third was where the body of Cassandra rested, and where Rand would be interred.

The guards put the stretchers down and looked around in awe. The only humans who had ever been down here were Dragon Keepers. Aswin sighed. "You four can head back now. We have some private rituals to perform. Thank you for your help."

"Really, we just go? Back up through the caves?" a guard asked, bewildered.

"Yes, just keep following this main path up. You'll eventually end up back in that main room. The stairs back up to the castle are on the end of the main hall. Don't turn down any side halls, or you will get hopelessly lost."

"Ahhh, okay," the guard said, worried.

Mila gave him her torch, pulling out an extra one she kept stuffed in her bag. She pulled out a scrap of paper and a small piece of charcoal, and handed it to her father. "Maybe sketch them a map to get out. We don't want them to die down here, do we?"

Her father nodded and made them a very rough sketch. He handed it over to the one who looked the smartest, and they thanked him and left. Aswin watched the four of them move up the path, holding the torch above them. He hoped they would be okay, but he needed privacy for what he was about to do. Finally, the light had disappeared, and he turned his attention to Alex.

He felt his pulse, still strong. Good. His breathing was shallow. Aswin propped him up and started rubbing his chest. He was trying to get the circulation flowing again. Mila sat on her haunches, looking at Alex with concerned eyes.

Aswin peeled up one of Alex's eyes, holding their torch close to look at them. The pupils were unseeing but responded to the light.

He considered the Prince, shaking his head. "I have no idea when he's going to wake up. Someone who takes just a few drops of noctom can sometimes sleep for a week. He's obviously had more than that. We are going to have to dribble water in his mouth, periodically, or he might just die from dehydration. We will need to keep him warm and move him every few hours so he doesn't develop sores."

"I will take care of him, father. I am his Dragon Keeper, after all."

"Nick moves to secure his power. Once he does wake, Alex will be in terrible danger," Aswin warned.

"What are we going to do?" Mila asked, filled with despair.

"We are going to get him out of Dumara, beyond the reach of his brother, and you are going to go with him," Aswin sighed.

"Why, Father? Why not go to Terrek?"

"It's not safe. Nick has been conspiring with Fresthav and Murdad. I fear war is coming. The best place for Alex is where there are no dragons. If he recovers, then he can return with an army and take back his throne. Until then, we will hide him. We will hide you."

"Me? I don't need to hide!" Mila exclaimed.

"You do. You and I are the Dragon Keepers. I refuse to be bound to Nick, and I suspect you share the same feelings. This is going to make him furious."

"Father," Mila said, fear gripping her heart, "What are you going to do?"

"Refuse to comply," Aswin said simply, turning to Rand's body. "But first, we must lay my friend to rest. I hope we will be able to ride with him to send him to the Dragon God, but that is doubtful."

"What will happen if we don't?"

"I'm not sure. Hopefully, he can find his way on his own," Aswin said sadly. He took his fingers and gently closed his friends' eyes for the last time and folded Rand's hands across his chest. He bent over and tenderly kissed his forehead. A single tear slipped from his eye, landing on the King's face. "Help me, Mila. We will put him next to Cassandra in the pit."

"And then what?" Mila asked, moving to take Rand's legs.

"And then we wait for darkness. If we take the lower entrance, we will come out near the bridge to the city. We will smuggle Alex and the egg to the shop and then go on from there."

———

Gayle and Linnea flew straight into a dragon battle with the rest of the winter dragons. They joined the nightfall dragons as they rampaged through the caves, dominating and crushing any opposition. Gayle was hit once by an errant beam of light from a drakaina's roar, but her leather plate armor absorbed the heat, leaving her only slightly singed.

Linnea's claws flashed as she got a sunrise drakaina up against the wall, and blood spilled. The sunrise drakaina fell to her belly in a submissive pose, a deep gash across her face. "Stay down!" Linnea roared, and the drakaina whimpered. All through the caves, the sunrise dragons submitted under the attack from the two clans.

"Stop! We surrender!" Robin, a warrior friend of Torrid's, roared. Four sunrise dragons, Holly, Mace, Tipps, and Rake lay dead in the main room.

Sumac hissed from where he had been hiding in a nearby nest. "Yes, we surrender."

Ibis and Kai stood, looking over the wounded and bleeding sunrise dragons, who all lay in submissive poses, not looking at the nightfall or the Fresthav dragons. Linnea lumbered over to Kai. "Hello, my love. Nice day for a bit of a fight, isn't it?"

"Oh yes, and how the mighty have fallen. Should we go find King Nick and pay our respects now?" Kai said.

"Yes, we really should. How rude of us," Linnea said. "Dragon Keepers. Take care of the wounded, all the wounded. I don't see Aswin or Mila. I wonder what Nick has done with them. Very curious."

"Of course," Gayle said, pulling out her astragenica and delivering it Linnea.

"Can you change Ibis and Kai for me?" Doyle asked. He was helping a sunrise dragon who was badly wounded.

"Yes, of course," Gayle said, pulling out two more bottles. She quickly poured them into their mouths and then ran over to Doyle to grab their clothes for them. Soon, Linnea, Kai, and Ibis stood in human form, looking around them.

"Take care of the wounded, please," Linnea demanded, heading toward the stairs with Ibis and Kia.

Gayle nodded. She wasn't sure she had enough supplies, but she would do her best.

Doyle was already moving among the dragons, looking at injuries. She joined him, and he glanced up at her. "Where do you think Aswin is? We could use his help."

"I don't know. Darius ran off to his brother's shop. Maybe they are there for some reason," she said. "Do you have any alcohol? We need to clean these wounds."

"I don't, but I suspect Aswin keeps some around here. Look around," he ordered, pulling out some healing balm.

———

In her nest, Sadie stirred. She longed to join the fighting, but she had been ordered to protect her egg. Two of her friends slipped into her room. "Sadie, the clan has been subdued."

"Good. Everything is going to plan. Has anyone smashed that egg yet?" she said, cradling hers protectively.

"No, we were just going there. Do you want to go with us?"

"I must not leave my egg. Nick would be furious with me."

"We will do the dirty work; we will return when it is done."

"Thank you, my friends. You will be rewarded for your loyalty."

"Of course, we are proud to serve the real King," they said, their dark red bodies flitting out of the cave.

———

A few nests down, Dahlia heard the commotion, but dared not leave her nest. She knew they would come for her egg, and she would be ready for them. She closed her eyes and prayed to the Dragon God for safe delivery of Alex and their unhatched son.

She didn't hear the two drakainas slip into her nest, she was so lost in her thoughts.

"She sleeps so peacefully," one said, sliding up close to her.

Dahlia's eyes flicked open. "Go away, Lor. You will not find what you are looking for here."

"What could you possibly mean, Dahlia?"

"I know why you are here. It's obvious. You are friends with Sadie."

"Give us the egg, Dahlia. Your husband is dead, Nick is King."

"No. I will not give you my egg." Dahlia said. She rose up on her hind eggs roaring, her claws outstretched. She swiped at Lor, who backed off.

"Her egg isn't there. I don't see it! What has she done with it?" Lor roared, backing away.

Dahlia's tail flipped in anger. "That's right. Come for me, girls. I can take you both. I am the daughter of Torrid!" she roared, light coming out of her mouth, hitting Lor in her flank. She whimpered and fled, leaving her friend staring at Dahlia with hatred.

"You're dead, Dahlia. We're telling Sadie what you have done."

"Bring it," Dahlia said, her tail twitching. "Maybe I'll go talk to her myself." She got out of her nest, full of rage. She stomped past the red dragon, who was looking at her in fear.

After Dahlia had passed her, she snuck up to the nest, just to make sure. No egg. What had Dahlia done with it? She looked throughout the cave, in every corner, but couldn't find the golden egg they knew existed.

———

Dahlia stomped through the hall, stopping in horror as she saw the winter dragons and the nightfall dragons throughout the place. She saw injured dragons everywhere.

A huge black dragon approached her, snarling. "Submit!" he demanded.

She roared back, "I will not submit. I am Dahlia, daughter of Torrid, mate of King Alex, and Queen of Dumara!"

At her words, three purple nightfall dragons approached her, along with two pale blue winter dragons. "My, what brave words for a woman whose mate is dead. You are not the Queen. Your throne is broken." Together, the three of them pushed against her, demanding she submit. She would not. She raised her head and roared, slashing at them.

This enraged the male dragons, so used they were to submissive drakainas. They all lunged at her, tearing and biting, but she fought savagely, her teeth and claws fighting for her life.

A laugh caused them to stop. Sadie, dark green, stood at the entrance to the nest. Her friends had come to report that they could not find Dahlia's egg.

"Where did you hide it, Dahlia?" Sadie said. She dared to leave her nest. Her friends were inside, and they could protect her egg, just for the moment. She could not resist watching her nemesis die.

"I will never tell you. You won't ever find it. It has been hidden by friends," Dahlia said, spitting and lunging. She could feel she was wounded. Blood dripped down her side.

Sunrise dragons were around her but dared not come to her aid. They were outnumbered, and the room was filled with their dead.

"We will find it. We will turn over every rock in every nest in this mountain. My son will be the only heir to the throne of Dumara."

"I loathe you, Sadie. You will never be Queen. The people will never accept you. I challenge you to a duel."

"A duel? Fine. It will be a duel then?"

"Right here, right now," Dahlia said, her eyes flashing.

Sadie rose on her hind legs and rushed forward, her teeth snapping. The nightfall and the winter dragons moved aside, watching with great interest. They had injured the sunrise dragon, but the one known as Dahlia was huge. Sadie, the summer dragon, wasn't as big or as muscular. They didn't know who would win in this fight. It seemed pretty evenly matched.

Dahlia roared, flipping her tail furiously at Sadie, hitting her in the right flank. Sadie scampered back and came harder, teeth bared and claws flying.

Dahlia swiped out a claw, hitting Sadie firmly across the chest. Sadie retreated a few steps and started pacing back and forth. Dahlia watched her, anticipating the next move.

But Sadie held back, scared. She had gotten herself into more than she could handle. She was not a fighter. She preferred to leave that to the male dragons.

Dahlia roared and lunged forward, grappling Sadie, her claws slashing at her back. Sadie tried to fight but ended up having to retreat again.

"You are no match for me, summer dragon and pretend Queen. I will crush you."

Sadie tried one more time, trying the tail slash move she had just seen Dahlia do, but she was too slow, and Dahlia pounced on her back, biting and slashing. Blood flew, and Sadie roared in pain, trying to throw her off. Eventually, she freed herself, but she was badly wounded. She retreated again and realized there was no way she could win.

The Dragon Keepers, Gayle and Doyle, stood watching the fight, waiting to help as soon as it was over. The sunrise dragons looked at Sadie with hatred in their eyes. They hated her with every fiber of their beings. They roared in encouragement to Dahlia as she stalked forward, intending to engage with Sadie.

Sadie looked at the five nightfall and winter dragons, watching from the sidelines. "I don't have time for this. Take her," she demanded.

At those words, a moment of fear flashed over Dahlia's face. The dragons descended on her while Sadie retreated, smirking.

Dahlia shrugged her shoulders and turned to face her attackers. She wouldn't win this fight, and she would probably die today, but she would injure as many as possible, and make them sorry they had ever messed with the daughter of Torrid.

As the caves shook with the ferocious roars, the rest of the sunrise dragons tried to look away, to hide their eyes, but they could not. Dahlia battled them with every ounce of her being, with every trick and technique her father had taught her, but she could not overcome five male warriors. She was burned by dark energy, and then frozen, as her light beam bounced off the walls. Finally, a nightfall dragon pinned her down, and then went for her jugular, ripping and tearing, and the daughter of Torrid died on the floor in a puddle of her own blood.

———

Down in the city, the soldiers from the castle retreated. The looters were simply too big. The main group had turned down Grand Avenue, and they could see flames rising and hear the shouts.

"Men, we've got to stop this. Let's cut over a few blocks and get ahead of them. We can create a barricade."

Just then, they were joined by squad C, who had been in charge of the dock area.

"Where have you been?" the commander demanded, pushing back his helmet. "We needed you!"

"We were clearing the docks. Most of the ships have left the harbor. The docks are secure."

"Well, that's all grand and good, but now the rioters are looting and burning Grand Avenue. We've got reinforcements, Murdad soldiers, holding the avenue leading to the castle, but we've got to end the rioting."

"We have been authorized to use force," the squad leader said, pulling out his sword.

"We may have to fight. Let's move out!" the commander shouted, pointing down Second, which was a residential street that ran parallel to Grand. They would try to cut off the rioters. It was their only option, or the entire city might burn.

———

Darius and Sam moved the heavy shelving unit to the front of the door. They could see the advancing mob and hear the smashing of glass.

"Here they come!" Darius yelled. "You two, get in the basement! Leave the door open! I'll hold them off here."

"I'm not leaving you here! Kiera, go to the basement!" Sam yelled, pointing to the door.

"NO! I'm not going!" She clutched a mop in her hands, her eyes fiery.

"I said GO!" Sam ordered. Kiera just pursed her lips and refused.

Sam sighed, and moved in front of her, but she resisted, moving in front of him.

"Stop it, you two! This is no time to squabble like children!" Darius roared. He was holding his staff in both hands, looking at the door. The mob was approaching, with not a sign of a soldier anywhere. "Incompetence," Darius mumbled.

They reached the tailor's shop first, and Kiera cried out as they broke the windows of her father's shop.

"He'll be okay!" Sam tried to assure her. He glimpsed Mr. Wright at the door, brandishing his sword and yelling, his face red. He lost sight of him as the mob surged into the shop. Soon, he saw people running out with bolts of fabric.

"Oh, no!" Kiera cried. "Do you think he's okay?"

"I see several people bleeding, so I think he put up a fight," Sam said, clutching his broom.

The mob turned their attention to the Dragon Keeper's shop,

yelling and pointing. Fear welled up in Sam, and he took a deep breath as the mob approached.

"Just to clarify, none of us are dying here today. If they want to steal health potions and healing balm, it's all theirs. The beauty of this place is that we can just make more," Darius said, gripping his staff.

"Of course. None of us are dying," Sam said, licking his lips.

A rock smashed through the window, breaking the glass into a thousand pieces. The rock landed at Kiera's feet, and she looked at it. Then she dropped her broom, picked up the rock, and heaved it back out the window. It hit a looter straight in his ugly face, and his nose exploded into a rain of blood.

"Good shot! That's my wife!" Sam yelled proudly, whacking another looter who was trying to crawl into the window with his broom. The man dropped back onto the sidewalk, holding his fingers.

Darius was staring at the door, mumbling an incantation. "FORTIS OSTIUM!" he said, blue light spilled from his staff, covering the door. His spell meant "Strong door." It wouldn't hold forever, but maybe long enough.

Looters still attempted to crawl through the window though, and together Sam and Kiera hit them with the mop and broom, thonking heads and pushing them away with the long handles. Soon, they were overwhelmed, and two burly-looking men crawled in, cutting themselves on the broken glass in the process, but they would not be deterred.

"FLAMMA!" Darius shouted, holding out his staff. Instantly, the two men alighted with flames and started screaming. They both dove back out the window, but they were replaced with three more men who crawled through. One of them pushed over the shelving that lined the storefront, and the shelf toppled over in a hail of broken potion bottles.

"We can't hold them off. There are too many. Get in the basement!" Darius ordered. Kiera and Sam, realizing that they would soon be outnumbered, headed straight for the door.

Darius turned to the looters. "Listen, take what you want. We don't care. The till is even full. It's all yours. We will just be downstairs, with the rats in the cold and damp. I'll even open the door for you." The men looked at him in incomprehension. He opened the door, and then backed away with his hands up, his staff help loosely in his left hand.

Another looter opened the door easily, looking at him like he was crazy. Sweating, Darius reached the basement stairs. "It's all yours. Take what you want. Till is full," he repeated, pulling the basement door shut. "FORTIS OSTIUM!" he repeated, and the blue light spilled out of his staff again, reinforcing the door.

With a sigh, Darius dropped the strong steel bolt across the door. What the looters didn't know was that his brother was a bit of a paranoid freak. This basement had a steel door with a thick bolt. With his spell in place, you would need a battering ram to take out this door. And with the bolt hole to the sewers, they could even escape if they had to.

Sam had already pushed back the shelves that hid the secret tunnel to the sewers. Kiara sat on a crate, looking scared.

"He was on fire," she whispered, looking at Darius with enormous eyes.

"I'm sure he's not dead, Kiera," Darius said, rolling his eyes. "It was either him or us."

The sound of crashing and laughter sounded from upstairs. They had probably found the till by now.

"How much was in the till, Sam?" Darius asked.

"About three hundred notes, and a bunch of change. Aswin doesn't like to keep a bunch of money in the till. It's all right down here," Sam said, looking at the crate Kiera sat on. Under it was the vault, filled with thousands and thousands of banknotes and gold coins.

Someone rattled the basement door. Banging sounded.

"Good try, boys, but that door isn't moving," Darius chuckled.

"What do we do now?" Kiera asked, wrapping her arms around her. It was cold down here.

"We are going to wait. Hopefully, they don't burn the building down."

Sam picked up a blanket from the supplies on the shelf and wrapped it around her. He kissed her forehead, and then sat down beside her, looking dejected.

"Do you think my parents are okay?" Kiera asked in a small voice.

"I don't know. I hope so," was all Sam said.

———

Torrid flew straight to Terrek, not even stopping when challenged by a patrol.

"I have important news! I must talk to King Cleon!" he shouted at them, and then the green dragons fell into formation beside him, flying with him straight to the castle.

He landed, and Tyson approached him. "Are you okay, sunrise dragon? You look spent."

"I need to speak to King Cleon immediately. Dumara is under attack!" Torrid said, his sides heaving.

From around him, the summer dragons mumbled. "I'll go get him right away," Tyson said.

A small boy stepped forward. "Hello, Dragon!" he spoke cheerfully. "I can't understand you yet, as I haven't been given my medallion, but you seem tired. Do you want an energy potion?"

Torrid looked at the small boy. This must be the Dragon Keeper's son. He thought an energy potion would be nice, so he opened his mouth wide. The boy popped the cork off the bottle with his teeth and poured it into Torrid's mouth with a smile. He chatted the whole time. "Sunrise dragons are so pretty. I love the golds and reds. Not that summer dragons aren't pretty. The emerald green color is my favorite. King Cleon is dark green, like an evergreen tree, but Queen Shayla is spring green. She looks like fresh grass."

Torrid listened as he felt the warmth of the energy potion flow

111

through him. He had never had one of these potions before, it was nice. One perk of being a King, he supposed. You got special treatment from the Dragon Keepers. He hoped that Aswin and Mila were safe, as he thought Nick would soon turn his attention to them. He couldn't really be King without a Dragon Keeper.

"Dragon of the sunrise. I heard you have an urgent message for me. What is the problem?" Cleon said, arriving at the bottom of the ascender. He threw off his clothes and quickly changed. Soon, he was standing before Torrid, in his dragon form, his dark green scales shimmering in the faint light of the caves.

"Your Majesty. I am Torrid, a warrior of the sunrise clan. I bring terrible news to you today. King Rand and his son Crown Prince Alex are dead."

"Dead?" Cleon asked in alarm, blinking his orange eyes. "What is going on?"

"Poison. Nick has seized power. We suspect he killed them. I slipped out as the nightfall dragons approached. Nick was working with them and has made some kind of deal. Our caves are overrun. I worry my friends are in danger, those that remain loyal to King Rand."

"This is terrible news, Torrid," Cleon said, pacing. "If Nick is working with Murdad, and perhaps Fresthav, their eyes will turn to me. We aren't safe!"

"Your daughter, Sadie, will be Queen," Torrid said, spitting. He hated her, and he did not hesitate to show his hatred, even to her father that stood before him.

"That is true. She will try to use her pull then, to deceive me, to lure me into a false sense of security."

"I would not drink anything she offered me," Torrid said, sarcastically.

"What can I do for you? Do you need sanctuary? I will shift my patrols to the east, but any sunrise dragon that needs it, will find sanctuary here."

"I must return to Dumara. My dragons are in danger, my

daughter is in danger. I will do what I can, where I can," Torrid said.

"You must be exhausted, you flew directly here as fast as you could," Cleon said. "Rest awhile before you go. Take a deer from our pile and restore your energy."

"Your young Dragon Keeper gave me an energy potion. I am fine. I will leave immediately. I may take you up on that meal, though," Torrid said, looking at the pile of fresh kill near the entrance. His mouth watered; he had not eaten today.

"Of course. Godspeed, Torrid. Thank you for the warning," Cleon said.

Torrid turned and made for the exit. He stopped at the kill pile and took the smallest deer he could find. He crunched the bones with his teeth and filled his belly. Then, he leapt into the sky and headed due west, toward the sunset, which was hiding now behind dark rain clouds.

Behind him, summer dragons took to the skies. They followed him to the border, and then stopped and circled. On Cleon's orders, they would run double patrols.

CHAPTER 10

A MIDNIGHT ESCAPE

In the basement, they heard the upstairs grow quiet. But still they stayed hidden.

"What time do you think it is? We've been down here for hours," Sam said, rubbing Kiera's shoulder. She had fallen asleep, her head resting on his chest. She awoke and rubbed sleep out of her eyes.

"I don't know. It was midafternoon when we came down here. It's been a few hours. Dark is probably coming," Darius said.

"Do you think it's safe to go upstairs?" Sam asked.

"I haven't heard anything for a while. The mob has probably taken everything and moved on," Darius said.

"We should peek out and see," Sam said, getting up.

"Yes, I need to find my brother. I wonder if he is in the caves," Darius said, joining him.

"I'm coming with you," Kiera said, standing and taking the blanket off. She picked up her mop from where she had left it.

"Oh, not this again," Darius rolled his eyes. He picked up his staff and crept up the stairs. He put his ear to the door, listening. He didn't hear a thing. He quietly lifted the bolt up and opened the door ever so slowly.

Night had fallen, and the moonlight spilled into the store. Laying on the floor were the bodies of two men, in a puddle of blood. The store had been ransacked, and nearly everything had been taken. The till lay smashed on the floor, completely empty. Glass covered everything, and nearly all the shelves had been tipped over.

He stepped out carefully, looking around for any hidden intruders. The front door was wide open, and he carefully stepped around the dead bodies and closed the door. The lock still worked, so he turned that, not that a person couldn't just climb through the broken windows.

Sam and Kiera had joined him, and they stood looking around. "Wow. They did a number on this place. What's up with these dead bodies? We didn't kill them," Sam asked, bending down. He turned one of the bodies over and saw the man had been stabbed through the heart.

Darius looked at the street. The street was lined with dead bodies, broken glass, bricks, and overturned carts. In the distance, a fire burned, but everything was silent.

He was startled to see a figure turn down the street, carrying a torch. It looked like a soldier; he wore the tunic of Dumara. Darius took a chance, "Sir! I am but a simple shopkeeper. We were hiding in our basement. Has the danger passed?" he shouted into the night.

The soldier quickly turned to the building, waving his torch across the front to see better. "You there! Are you safe?"

"I think so. We just have a lot of damage here on the inside, but no injuries to our person. There are a few dead men here, but they are looters, and we didn't kill them," Darius said, slipping back a few steps, so the soldier's torch would not illuminate his face.

"We've secured the city. There was a lot of fighting on this street. The riots have broken up, the looters are dead, in the dungeons, or they slipped back to their rat holes down near the docks. Curfews in place. No going out, stay inside, and board up if you can. We will patrol the city, and keep order," the soldier said, trying to get a look at the man.

"Thank you, sir. We will stay inside," Darius said.

The man moved on, and Darius turned to Sam and Kiera. "Let's look upstairs, make sure no one's hiding out."

They crept upstairs and found that the place had been ransacked. Mila's room was torn up, her jewelry box missing, and they had even taken some of her clothing. They must have been looking for money, because the bed had been cut, the feathers strewn everywhere.

Aswin's room fared no better. His wardrobe was empty, his clothes scattered across the floor.

"Well, they didn't find the goods. Everything's a mess, but this can all be cleaned up. Lord knows my brother has enough money downstairs in the safe to rebuild this place over 10 times if needed."

"They left the food. I guess they didn't want day old bread and some wrinkly apples. Oh, and beans, of course," Sam said, peeking into the bean canister.

Kiera was gathering firewood that had been scattered across the floor. She stacked a few pieces into the wood stove and then looked for the matches. They were gone. "They left beans, but took the matches?"

"Here, let me," Darius said, lowering his staff. "Flamma," he intoned, and fire came out of the stone set on the top of his staff, igniting the dry wood.

Kiera looked out the window to her parents' shop across the street. The windows upstairs were not broken, but there was no sign of life inside. "We've got to go see if they are okay."

"Okay, let's go," Sam said, picking up his broom.

Darius sighed and looked across the street. He supposed he should go with these two. They were bound to hurt themselves with cleaning equipment if given the chance.

Just then, thunder boomed in the distance. "Storm's coming," Darius said, "Let's hurry."

———

Deep in the crypt, they had laid Rand to rest, wrapping him in a sheet, and letting him slip into the family crypt. They turned to Alex, and Aswin slipped some more capsicum under his tongue. He looked at the egg, tapping it a few times. It rocked slightly. "It's still good," he said, tucking it more firmly between Alex's legs.

"You're going to be okay to help carry this stretcher, Mila?" Aswin asked.

"I'm going to have to be, aren't I? If I need to, I can stop to rest." She sighed and readjusted her bag.

"We are going to head for the lower entrance. It's nearby and rarely used," Aswin said. Together, they picked up the stretcher and started moving through the caves.

Mila had to rest several times, and her hands were blistering. She cursed Alex for being so heavy. He was probably at least 220 pounds of muscle. Every time they put the stretcher down, they did so gingerly, not wanting to chance breaking the egg.

Finally, they made it to the lower entrance. Night had fallen. Thunder boomed in the distance, and the night was dark as ink.

"Rain is coming," Aswin said, looking at the sky. He looked up the mountain behind him, but everything was dark. He could make out some shapes of dragons in the skies above him as the lightning flashed in the distance, and he ducked back inside the caves.

"Dragons up above. They look like nightfall dragons. What are they doing here? This is bad," Aswin said.

"They will see us from above. This white sheet sticks out like a sore thumb. It's like waving a flag. Here I am!" Mila said, pulling it off.

Luckily, Alex had been wearing his dark riding pants. But his favorite white linen shirt gleamed. Aswin pulled off his cloak and draped it over him. Just then, the skies opened up, and a drenching rain hammered down. The thunder and lightning flashed in the distance.

"No time like now," Aswin said, "Are you good? We won't be able to stop for a while."

"I'll make it work," Mila said, setting her mouth in a firm line. She didn't care if her hands bled, she would carry Alex wherever he needed to go.

"Okay, let's move out. Move fast but be careful," Aswin said. "The path is flat here, but narrow. It lets out just by the bridge across the river."

The opening to the caves was concealed behind a niche, and they stepped out into the pouring rain. Instantly, Mila was drenched to the bone. They made their way carefully down the path, going slowly so as not to trip. They made their way to the bridge, and Aswin looked around. The streets were quiet, but then another clap of thunder nearly caused him to jump out of his skin. People were staying inside because of the rain.

They made their way quickly through the streets. Aswin paused under a broken awning for a minute, and they gently lowered Alex to the ground. Just a few more blocks and he would be home.

"Father, the windows are broken out," Mila said, worry creeping into her voice.

"And everything is dark. There has been trouble here," Aswin said.

They picked the stretcher back up and then made their way down Grand Avenue. As they got to the merchant shops, they noticed dead people in the streets, laying with their blank eyes staring into the sky. Here and there were even dead soldiers, and a barricade made with overturned wagons, where most of the fighting must have occurred.

"I hope Sam is okay. I hope our neighbors are okay," Mila worried. Her muscles were on fire, and she had a stitch in her side. Her entire body was sore, and she almost felt like she needed a stretcher herself.

Eventually, they reached their store, and it was dark. "The windows are broken, Hades. Something bad happened here," he said, as they sat Alex down on the sidewalk gently. He fumbled for the door. Strangely, he found it locked, and he reached into his pocket to find his key.

———

Across the street, the trio entered the tailor's shop cautiously. Like the Dragon Keeper's shop, everything was in shambles.

"Father? Mother?" Kiera cried out. She heard a groan from the back room and started to rush forward, but Darius grabbed her arm.

"Carefully," he cautioned.

They stepped over mountains of fabric, left piled on the floor. Their machines had been smashed, and of course, the till was empty.

Laying between the large sewing machines was the body of Franklin Wright, stabbed with his own sword.

"Father! NO!" Kiera rushed forward. She shook him, but his eyes remained staring to the sky. "I told you not to be a hero! Look what they have done to you, and for what? A few bolts of fabric!" she cried. Sam touched her shoulder, and she threw herself into his arms. He awkwardly patted her back.

Meanwhile, Darius had moved to the back room. It looked like a workroom for piecing together fabrics and cutting out patterns. Judith Wright laid on the table, naked. She had been stabbed with a pair of her own scissors, but she was still alive. Her head turned to look at him, full of fear, and her hand reached out to him. "Help me," she pleaded.

He rushed forward. Judith had been assaulted, and left for dead, the scissors buried deep into her shoulder. "Sam!" Darius yelled, "Sam! I need help!"

Sam disengaged himself from Kiera and left her sobbing over her father. He investigated the back room, afraid of what he would find.

"Mrs. Wright!" he exclaimed, rushing forward.

"Franklin tried to stop them. He killed a few of them with his

sword, but they killed him, and then they drug me back here and
…" Her voice broke. "I thought I was dead, but here I am. I can't
move, though. The scissors went all the way through, and it hurts
to move." She reached up a shaking hand to touch the handle of
the scissors.

Her face was bloody. Darius looked around and found a piece
of heavy felt on the floor.

Kiera came looking for them, her eyes red. "Mother!" she
exclaimed, tears pouring down her red face.

Darius covered Judith with the felt. "We've got to move her. We
can take her across the street, and I can work on her. I'm worried
about bleeding when we take those sheers out though."

"The looters took all the supplies, but we've got plenty of stock
stored in the basement. We can put together a little workshop down
there for now," Sam said.

"Okay, Judith. I'm going to put a minor spell on you. Just until I
free you from this table, okay?" Darius said, looking at the woman
before him.

"Okay," she sighed with relief.

He moved forward, bringing out his staff. "SOMNUM," he
intoned, and the blue light surrounded her. Her eyes became heavy,
and she drifted off.

"We have to hurry. Here, use this to stop the bleeding when he
pulls her free." He gave a handful of fabric he had found on a side
table to Kiera. It was a curtain she and Judith had been working
on, for their future home. It was a blue and white checkered
pattern, and her heart broke as she held it ready.

"I'm going to take this shoulder, and you on the other side,
Sam. On three, we will pry her up," Darius ordered.

"Okay," Sam said with uncertainty. He was glad Darius had
knocked her out. He didn't know if he could stand hurting
Judith.

"One, two, three," Darius said, and with a yank, they both
pulled on her shoulders. With a pop, the shears holding her to the
table wrenched free, and a stream of blood flowed down her bare

back. Kiera quickly moved to press the fabric against it. Sam held Judith in his arms as her eyes fluttered open again.

"Oh, it hurts," she moaned, sobbing.

"Can you stand, Judith?" Darius asked, prompting her. He had to get her back across the street. As soon as he got her fixed up, he had to go looking for his brother. He had not expected to be delayed so long from his objective.

He helped her rise to her feet, and she was unsteady. Sam moved to her left side and supported her, nearly dragging her along. They made their way out of the back room. At the sight of her husband, dead on the floor, Judith nearly collapsed in grief.

"He's gone, Mom. We will come back and give him a proper burial," Kiera said as she turned her head away.

"I know. I can't believe it. Why did he have to be the hero?" Judith wailed.

They hurried to the front, having difficulty making their way through the torn-up room.

Lightning flashed, and the rain poured down. The streets ran red from the blood spilled today. A dark figure stood in the doorway, and a familiar voice rang out.

"Brother. I didn't expect to find you here," Aswin said, his voice rang out above sound of the storm.

———

Mila and Aswin had already moved Alex inside. He was in the basement, resting on a makeshift cot, covered with blankets, still nearly dead, but not quite.

They moved Judith downstairs as well, shoving over a few crates to give her a place to lie on the floor. Mila ran upstairs and found one of her nightgowns on the floor, and grabbed the quilt and her pillow from the pile of debris. She lugged it back downstairs and found her father mumbling as he dug through an opened crate.

They were fast running out of room in the small basement. "Tomorrow, I'll see if I can board up the windows, and then we can move back upstairs," Sam said, holding a glass of water up for Judith to drink from.

"I could go back up to the apartment and make a pot of beans," Mila offered, searching for a way to be helpful.

"I need you down here. But that's a good idea. Kiera, could you handle dinner for us? We will come get you when we are done with your Mom, okay?"

Kiera looked scared. She got up, shaking. "Yes, of course. Is she going to be okay?"

"I'll be fine, dear," Judith said, closing her eyes against the pain.

"I'll go with you," Sam said as he brushed his trousers off as he rose. Mila moved to take his spot, supporting Judith on her good side.

The couple left, with Sam throwing a concerned look behind him.

Aswin sighed and placed a pack of herbs on the top of the crate. "Judith, I'm going to have to pull those shears out. You're probably going to lose a lot of blood, but I'll try to work quickly. We are going to have to sew fast. This is where I'll need Mila's help. She can hold the wound closed while I stitch."

"I can't believe I'm going to allow Aswin Fletcher to sew me up," Judith said with a pained chuckle. "I thought we made an agreement years ago; you would leave all the sewing to me."

"Ahh, Judith. I know. I'm sorry dear, you're going to have to trust me with this one."

Mila brushed her hair back, and Judith sighed and rested her head on her shoulder. "You're so much like your mother, Mila. I miss her."

Aswin's eyes flicked to Darius, and words flew between the two unspoken. Finally, Darius spoke up. "I came today to find you, brother. Nick showed up in Fresthav and promised Linnea all sorts of things I'm sure he can't deliver. The dragons flew to the caves and met up with nightfall. I fear for the sunrise dragons."

"Thank you, I think. But it was your poison that killed King

Rand and almost killed Alex here. You got any ideas about that? He's out cold," Aswin said, waving at the body of the Prince.

Darius moved over to him. He had noticed the body of the Prince, but honestly did not know what Aswin planned to do with it. Frankly, he had thought the man was dead. He felt for a pulse and found it strong under his fingers. His body was warm, but it was true. The man might as well be a corpse.

"Just so you know, I did not know that noctom was going to be used like this. Kai showed up with Doyle about six months ago and demanded I make it for him. I gave it to him with a warning, but I thought he just wanted to scry. I had no idea it would end up in Nick's hands, or I would have never given it to him. How much noctom do you think he got?" Darius asked, pulling up the eyelids and looking at his pupils.

"The teapot was half full. King Rand must have had the full dose. He was dead nearly instantly, and there was froth around his mouth, so he convulsed. Alex was lying on his side, with his eyes open. Maybe a mouthful? Or perhaps just a sip. It couldn't have been that much, or he would be dead."

"But enough to knock him out in an instant. Oh, I expect he's having wonderful visions. He should write them down when he wakes up," Darius said. "The last time I used noctom, it was just the residuals left in a pot, and I slept for three days. He's going to sleep for a while. Make sure you try to give him some water at some point."

"Yeah, that's what I told Mila." Aswin said. Searching, he found what he was looking for, an extra set of smaller sized dragon bone needles. "Judith, we're going to start. Are you ready?"

"Ready as I'll ever be," she said weakly.

"I can put her to sleep again, but it won't last long," Darius offered.

"No, don't bother. I'll endure."

"Here then, bite down on this," Aswin said, handing her a slim piece of wood used for kindling. She put it in her mouth and closed her eyes.

"Okay, Mila! Ready?" Aswin asked, looking at her, a needle in one hand and a flask of iseiki in the other.

"Yeah, let's do this," Mila said. She reached over and, in one swift movement, yanked out the shears.

With a scream muffled only by the stick in her mouth, Judith nearly rose from the floor. Working quickly, Aswin splashed the alcohol into the wound, and she screamed again.

He stitched up the wound quickly as Mila held the cloth ready. Soon, he was done on the first side, and then he repeated the process on the other.

When he was done, Judith lay gasping, tears of pain fresh on her cheeks. Aswin passed her some willow bark powder, and Mila dumped it into a glass of water. "Drink. This will help with the pain."

Mila sat Judith up, and then helped her into the nightgown. Darius had made up a bed next to Alex, and Mila helped Judith lay gently down on her good side and covered her with a blanket.

"I'll go get Kiera. I'm sure she wants to comfort you," Mila said gently.

"Thank you, Mila. Thank you all for everything you've done," Judith said with tears in her eyes.

———

Upstairs, Kiera stopped stirring the beans when she heard her mother scream. She turned to flee down the stairs, but Sam stopped her. "You'll only get in the way. Let them work. They will be done soon," he said softly.

A few minutes later, Mila appeared at the top of the stairs. "It's done. She's resting. We got it out and cleaned out the wound pretty good. I'll watch the beans. Go to your mother."

Kiera choked back a sob and rushed down the stairs. Mila stood stirring the beans, looking pensively at the rain out the window. The storm had moved past, and now it was just a light rain.

"You're amazing, Mila Fetcher," Sam said, a touch of sadness in his voice.

"I know, Sam," she said sadly, looking at the dead corpses in the street.

———

Aswin and Darius left the basement, leaving Kiera to watch over the patients. Aswin pulled up a stool and looked over the ruins of his shop.

"This is a mess," Aswin said with a sigh.

"That it is," Darius acknowledged.

"I need to go check on the dragons. I'm worried about them." Aswin looked up at the mountain. "But I also need to plan."

"Plan what?"

"I need to find a ship to take Alex to Norda. It's our only hope."

"What do you mean, Norda?"

"There are no dragons in Norda. He can rest and recuperate there. When he gets his wits about him, he can take back Dumara from Nick."

"Well, that's a colossal task. How's he going to do that?" Darius said, chuckling.

"I don't know, but I'm not sending him empty-handed," Aswin said. "I'm sending Mila with him. It will get her away from Nick. I'll send her my fortune. Alex can use it to hire mercenaries, buy some ships, smooth things over."

"Wow. The tightfisted Aswin Fletcher is going to give up his fortune on a long shot? Okay then, say you make all that happen. What's next for you? Isn't Nick going to demand your service?"

"Oh, he can demand anything he wants. Whether he gets my service is another matter," Aswin said, fire coming into his eyes.

"You're mad. He'll have your head," Darius said tilting his head and considering his brother.

"Oh, I think not. He needs me." Aswin smiled.

"I don't understand, Aswin."

"It's the least I can do for my old friend," Aswin said, thinking of how he lowered Rand into the crypt, well before his time. Bitterness filled his mouth, and he thought of how he wanted Nick dead. That would have to wait. He had very important tasks to do as quickly as possible. "Come with me, brother. I need your help to find a captain."

"At this hour? Are you mad?" Darius said, looking at the clock.

"Dad, the beans are done," Mila called from the top of the stairs.

"Well, we can eat first, and then we must be off," Aswin said, rising. Darius followed him, shaking his head. He would try to go to the caves tomorrow to see if Gayle was okay. He was worried about her.

———

Aswin made up his mind to use the sewers to get to the docks, and to take Alex and Mila with him. It was getting late, and sunrise would be here before he knew it. He wanted to be in the caves before the sun came up, to see what he could do to help.

Mila quickly packed what she could, and Sam repacked her Dragon Keeper's bag. He didn't know what she could find in Norda, so he filled the top with all the raw herbs and ingredients he could. Aswin opened his vault, pulling out bag after bag of gold and silver. He left the banknotes; they would be all but useless in Norda.

"Sam, I'm going to need you to carry the gold. Mila will take the bags, and Darius and I will take the stretcher."

"What about the egg, father? Should we take that with us?" Mila asked, looking at the golden egg laying between Alex's legs.

He considered for a moment, his mind spinning. It would be hard for them to conceal, and it might be broken on the ocean voyage. "It might be better to hide it here, but we will need to keep it warm."

127

"I'll take care of it," Sam volunteered. Kiera gathered the egg gently in her arms, wondering at its beautiful colors.

Aswin nodded. "You and Kiera can move upstairs. With Mila gone, we will have extra space. Judith can stay here with us as long as she needs. Put the egg behind the woodstove, hide it in the wood box. It will be warm and safe there."

They moved out, Sam straining from the weight of the treasure, Mila struggling with two bags. The door to the sewer had been opened, and water rushed past them, full of rainwater from the streets above. Aswin knew it ran straight down the middle of Grand, before turning and running in an even larger tunnel down to the harbor. The sewer had a narrow two-foot-wide berm on the edge, which they walked carefully single file down. Darius tapped his staff on the stone. "LUX LUME!" he declared, and the arching vault of the sewer was lit by the glowing tip of his staff.

"Here, Mila, I'm going to need both hands. Just hold it out. The spell will remain active until you tap the staff on the rock again."

"Okay," she said hesitantly, holding the staff in front of her. It seemed to throb with power and left her hand feeling strange.

They moved through the sewers, the floors slippery and wet, the rushing water just inches from their feet. They turned right, and now they were traveling under South Street, heading for the harbor. The vaults here opened as the channel widened and the water rushed even faster.

It seemed like hours and hours, but it hadn't really been that long when they reached the end of the tunnel. Just ahead, a thick gate blocked the entrance, allowing the water out, but keeping out curious humans. A service door was set in the side, but it was locked with a heavy padlock, which looked new. They sat Alex in a small room just off the entrance, and then Aswin turned to the gate, giving it a firm shake. "Hmmm, that wasn't there before."

"I've got this," Darius said, taking his staff from Mila. He tapped it on the floor to extinguish the flame, then commanded,

"APERTA CINNE!" The lock snapped open, and Darius grinned. "I did my part, now what, brother? You're the man with the plan."

"I'm going to hire a ship captain. It should be easy, right?" Aswin said, stepping out to the sandy beach. Just to the right of him were the docks, and his face fell.

"Where are the ships?" Darius said, looking at row after row of empty slips.

"They're all gone! The harbor was full yesterday!" Aswin lowered his head, feeling hopeless. All was surely lost.

"Wait, I see one ship at the end. Way down in the first slip." Darius pointed down the beach.

Aswin looked up, hope in his eyes, and then his heart sank, when he saw it wasn't flying a flag. "What kind of ship is that? It's not flying any flag."

"Well, there is only one way to find out. Let's go ask."

"Right now? Is there anyone on that boat? It looks dark," Aswin said, squinting down the docks. He hadn't seen it because the boat looked abandoned. It wasn't a huge ship, and the docks were empty.

"You're the one who wanted to come down to the docks at midnight. I don't know why you thought this would work out. Of course, all these sailors are asleep. It's midnight."

"It sounded better in my head. Now we are just going to walk up to a dark, unknown ship and ask them for passage to Norda. What was I thinking?" Aswin asked, shaking his head.

"Well, you were thinking you had half a dead man to offload before daylight. I'm sure someone is going to come looking for you shortly. So, let's get hopping. I need to go find Gayle."

"Gayle, as in the Dragon Keeper of Fresthav?"

"The one and only, we are together now," Darius said with a grin.

Aswin shook his head. He didn't know what was going on with his brother, but he was acting like a changed man, looking out for others, showing a little empathy. Who knew he had it in him?

They scrambled down the beach, hoping against hope someone

could help them. Mila and Sam waited in the dark sewer with a treasure of gold, and a nearly dead King sleeping at their side.

———

Up in the castle, Nick paced, watching the storm roll over the city. The dragons were patrolling the skies. He would go down to the caves soon, but he had a problem, he had no Dragon Keeper. He could turn into a dragon with no problem, but to turn back into his human form was where the issue was. He supposed he could borrow a potion from Doyle or Gayle, but he didn't want to be put in that position. Ibis or Linnea could easily snatch his throne, keeping him trapped in his dragon form if they desired, and he knew that after they had been subdued, he would not have the backing of the sunrise dragons. They would kill him if given half a chance. His small band of friends were no match for Torrid and his warriors.

He turned to look at the city. He had been taking reports all day from the guard. Linnea had come upstairs earlier with Gayle to report that Dahlia was dead, and the egg could not be found. The last anyone had seen, it had been in Dahlia's nest. She also reported that Aswin and Mila had briefly visited Dahlia before taking the bodies of his brother and father to the crypts.

He suspected Aswin might know where the egg was. He wouldn't put it past the man to take the egg and hide it. Well, he would find the Dragon Keeper, and he would find the egg. If he had to, he would torture Mila in front of her father's eyes until he crumbled. Then, he would bind Mila to him.

Gayle had confirmed to him that Darius was around here somewhere. It amused him that she averted her eyes, and he knew that scoundrel of a sorcerer and her were romantic items. Well, maybe he could use that to his advantage. Fresthav was in his corner, after all. He would force a binding if he had to, but he wanted a Dragon Keeper of his own.

The riots and looters had been put down. There had been a lot of damage to the Grand Avenue shops, but that could all be rebuilt. He would send wagons out to collect the dead. As a sign of goodwill, he would send carpenters out to help the shopkeepers board up their broken windows. It was the least he could do.

But the first thing he would do was send his entire company of soldiers out, to find the Dragon Keepers and the sorcerer. It was his utmost priority.

CHAPTER 11

THE SOUTHERN PEARL

Captain Gideon Booker of The Southern Pearl was cross. He had been stuck in the godforsaken port of Dumara for the entire winter. He was running out of money, and his boat still wasn't fixed.

They had arrived in late fall and had been scheduled to pick up a shipment of iron ore. Unfortunately, they ran into a bit of a problem just a few days before they reached the port. Their main mast has broken in the storm, tearing the mainsail and all its rigging. Luckily, they had chopped the mast free before it took the ship to the bottom of the sea. Their ship's carpenter had nearly given up, but he had managed to jury-rig the remaining two masts the best he could. It still sailed, but it was much slower than before, and it wouldn't hold up in the storms of winter.

Over the winter, the mast had been repaired, and new sails were ordered. But they had lost their load and hadn't been able to find another one before the winter storms arrived.

Now it was spring, and he had a hold full of fine wine to take back to the port of Hattirus, but he had run out of coin.

Gideon couldn't leave the docks legally until he had paid his docking fees from the winter. Normally, he would have just slipped out in the dead of night, but the harbormaster was holding his sails hostage until he paid up.

He slammed down another shot. He was going to have to ask the harbormaster for a loan, and the man would gladly give him one, but he would expect it to be paid in full plus more the next time he came to town. There was no way to make money, and he was already in the hole from this trip. He just couldn't win.

He looked at his first mate, his partner, good old Norman, who smiled and refilled the glass. "Oh, not that bad. It's just money. We will pay a visit to the harbormaster tomorrow, butter him up a little and plead poverty, and he'll give us back our sails."

"I hate that man," Gideon slurred and took another shot. He had probably had enough. He got up and stumbled over to his bunk, where he promptly passed out, only to be shaken awake a few hours later.

"I know it's late and you are two sheets to the wind, but we have a visitor."

"What time is it? Who visits at midnight?" Gideon mumbled.

"I know, I know. But he's got gold, lots of gold, and all he wants is passage for two souls."

"Gold, you say? By all means, show him in. The Dragon God might have just answered our prayers," he mumbled, running a hand through his long black hair. He looked thoroughly disreputable, half-drunk, last night's dinner stained on his front. But he slipped on his boots and stumbled out to the galley. His men were sleeping below, but the night guard stood with two rich-looking blokes who appeared to be brothers. One was carrying a small bag of gold, and the other had a long, strange-looking staff.

"What do you two want? Don't you know I was sleeping?" Gideon mumbled.

Norman nodded. "But they've got gold," he pointed out.

"My name is Aswin Fletcher, and this is my brother, Darius," the man with the gold began. "Listen, I know this is an odd request, at an odd time at night, but we are in a bit of a jam."

"Yeah, aren't we all? What can I help you with?"

134

"Well, it's complicated. We need your help."

"Well, spit it out. I ain't got all night," Gideon mumbled, looking at the gold.

"What my brother is trying to say is that we need passage for his daughter, and errrr, her husband. They got into a spot of trouble with the King, and they need to be gone as soon as possible," Darius said.

"Ha. That's good. You heard the King's dead, right?"

"Yes. The trouble is with King Nick. You saw the rioting on the streets today? It's all part of that," Aswin said.

"Ahh, I see. Got himself caught leading a riot, I take it? And where are these troublemakers?" Gideon asked. He didn't see any daughter or husband.

"Well, that's the problem. They are hiding down the beach. Her husband is well, a little sick. He got knocked around a little while in custody. We managed to free him, but he's a little out of it. So to say. We need you to take them to Norda. Is this ship a Norda ship? It looks like it – small, light, three masts for the open waters," Darius said, scanning the bones of the ship.

"You know your ships. We are a Norda ship. I'm Captain Gideon Booker, and this is my first mate, Norman."

"Are you leaving soon?" Aswin asked, his eyebrows raised.

"As soon as possible. I would have left yesterday, when the soldiers came down and warned us, but I have problems of my own. Now, let's discuss the cost of passage. It sounds like your daughter and her husband are in a bit of a tight spot. You look like a well-off man. You've apparently got a bag of gold. I don't know how much is in there, but it looks like it will do. Food and board and a fast trip to Norda with no questions asked."

Aswin looked down at the bag, and he held it out, reluctantly. "There is 300 gold in this bag. I expect you to leave as soon as possible, before the morning light, if you can manage it. And I bring them aboard now."

"Great. Sounds like a plan. I'll be happy to do this little errand for 300 gold," Gideon said, reaching out his hand.

"Great. We will go get them now. My daughter's husband is on a stretcher."

"Great, a helpless woman and an incapacitated man. At least they will stay out of my way," Gideon mumbled.

Aswin turned to him, "Don't you underestimate my daughter. She has the blood of dragons, and her husband will eat you alive."

"Okay, then. Sorry, sorry if I offended you. What are their names, or should I just call them dragonborn?"

Darius started laughing, choking, really. "Mila and Allen."

"Okay then, sounds great. I'll try to avoid impeding the dragons," Gideon said. He turned to Norman. "We got a spare cabin to put these yahoos in?"

He sighed, "Not really. They can have mine, but then we have to bunk together."

"Thank you, Norman. Always willing to go the extra mile for your captain," Gideon said with a sly grin.

Norman blew him a kiss and gave him a wink before leaving with Aswin and Darius.

Gideon looked at all his shiny new coins. Half of it would go to the harbormaster, and the other half would keep him and Norman afloat until they could get another load in Hattirus.

———

Mila was sitting next to Alex, holding his hand.

Sam had been staring down the sewer into the darkness. He glanced back over at her. "Thank you, Mila."

She had been staring into the darkness, thinking, and his voice startled her. "For what?"

"For introducing me to Kiera. For putting a good word in with your father. I have a life now. Before, I was just a dumb kid."

"Oh, Sam," Mila said, shaking her head. "I'm scared. What if Alex never wakes up?"

"I'm sure he will, and you'll be fine, Mila. I have no doubt."

Her father and uncle stumbled in. "We've made some

arrangements. Let's go!" Aswin said urgently. "There was a soldier on the dock patrolling, but we avoided him. He went up Second Street, so hopefully we won't see him again."

Aswin and Darius picked up the stretcher, and Mila gathered her bags. With a groan, Sam picked up the bags of coins, his muscles protesting. He would feel this tomorrow, for sure.

They made their way down the beach, huffing and puffing with their heavy loads through the sand. Finally, they made it to the ship and were met by the captain, who grinned down at them.

"Ahhh, there are my guests. I'm Captain Gideon Booker. Welcome to The Southern Pearl. My ship is small, but my hulls are full. We leave as soon as my first mate comes back with my sails. I've already woken my men!"

"Thank you, I'm Mila Fletcher, This is Alex."

"Allen. Your husband, Allen," Darius coughed. They had forgotten to tell her about the pseudonym.

"Oh, yes," Mila said, looking at her . . . husband?

Gideon caught it and raised an eyebrow. "Well, whoever he is, welcome aboard. I'll show you your cabin, and then you must excuse me. I've got to prepare to leave."

He led them to a tiny room just off the main deck. It had one bunk, a desk, and a chest of drawers. The bed was stripped, but a blanket and linens and a pillow were on the end of the bed. "Breakfast is before dawn, but not today. We've got to leave. Dinner is at sunset. That's it."

"Thank you," Mila said firmly, and he left, glancing at Sam and his bags of gold.

Sam plunked the bags of gold on the deck, and Aswin and Darius put Alex down. Mila quickly made the bed, and then they transferred him onto the top of it.

"I guess these can go in the drawers. It's not like you have a lot of clothes," Sam said, opening the bottom drawer. He stuffed the bags in the bottom.

Mila covered them with one of her shirts and shook her head. "Not exactly secure, but it will have to do."

"I have one thing to do before you leave," Darius said, with a glint in his eye. He held out his staff and started mumbling. The jewel on the end of his staff started glowing purple, and the room was filled with the light, casting strange shadows. "Serenum!" he shouted, and the light pulsed out. It went through the entire ship, pulsing just once as it spread up and out into the sky, but it happened in an instant, and the sailors on the deck rubbed their eyes and blinked, thinking their lack of sleep was playing tricks on their minds.

"What did that do?" Mila tilted her head and looked at her uncle. He was always full of mysteries.

"It was a spell for fair weather. Can't chance a freak storm will come and take you to the bottom of the sea, especially with the storms we've had the past several days." Darius looked at his staff, pensively.

"Daughter, give me a hug. Please," Aswin pleaded, holding out his arms.

Mila fell into her father's arms, and he hugged her tightly, tears coming to his eyes. He kissed her forehead. "I don't know when we will meet again. Be safe."

She nodded. "What should we do once we get to Norda?"

"I can't tell you that. You'll have to work it out as you go. I can tell you, they hate dragons, so Alex will have to stay in human form once he wakes up. You have a treasure in that drawer. My life savings. It should help you along the way. Maybe let things cool down, sneak back into Terrek. King Cleon will probably help you if he is able."

"Father, what will become of you? You said you wouldn't serve Nick."

"I won't serve him. I expect we will have a strongly worded discussion. He may kill me, but I doubt it. With you gone, he will need me more than ever."

"You be safe then," Mila said, her eyes flashing.

"Hey, I want a hug, too," Darius said, holding out his arms. Mila laughed and turned to her uncle. She gave him a squeeze.

138

"What are you going to do?" she asked while her uncle patted her back awkwardly.

"Unfortunately, part of this whole mess is because I made that noctum. I feel bad. And because my brother is going to be difficult and not comply with Nick, he's probably going to want me to bind him to a new Dragon Keeper."

Their eyes turned to Sam. He was the obvious choice. "What, me?" his voice squeaked.

"If Mila is gone, and I won't do it, who else knows anything about dragons?" Aswin said, looking at his shopkeeper sadly.

"Well, I won't do it. I won't be able to," Darius said. He pulled back and resumed looking at his staff. It was part of him and had been for a very long time. He sighed, and quickly, he removed the veta stone from the top and handed it to Mila. "Keep this safe. I want it back someday if possible." He then took his staff, and with no further hesitation, broke it in two over his knee. He dropped the pieces on the floor, and then crossed his arms, looking at them firmly.

"Did you just break your staff?" Aswin said, awe in his voice.

"Yeah. I can make another one easily. I just need a bit of wood. And I don't technically need that stone, but that stone amplifies power. But what Nick doesn't know won't hurt him, will it? Can't bind a new Dragon Keeper to him if I don't have my staff, can I?"

Sam looked scared. "He'll still come for me, won't he?"

"Yes, probably, but you won't have to deal with him being in your head. Gayle has found it to be a huge problem with Thora. The only way she can get a moment of privacy is to drink herself drunk. You don't seem like a drinking man, Sam."

"I'm not," he said, gulping.

"Okay then. Are we ready?" Aswin said, turning to the door.

"Wait! I didn't get a hug!" Sam said, frantically reaching for Mila.

"Oh, Sam!" Mila said, holding out her arms.

He gave her a squeeze and then laughed. "Mila, I don't know what the future holds, but I know Kiera and I will be here, holding down the fort, so to speak. We are going to live in the shop, so when you return, come find us."

"I will Sam. You tell Kiera goodbye for me and tell her she had better take care of herself. I expect to meet my honorary niece or nephew, and Alex's son, when we return."

"Of course. I will. I promise," Sam said, "Although I do not know how to raise a dragon."

They all laughed, and after one last round of goodbyes, the group left the cabin. As they exited the boat, they noticed the first mate, Norman, had returned. He was yelling at a surly group of sailors, angry at having been roused out of their hammocks so late in the night.

They had sails spread out on the deck along with piles of ropes and rigging. The flag of Norda had been run up, and it snapped in the wind.

"Now, we need to head to the caves. I need to see what Nick has done," Aswin said, fire in his eyes.

"And I'm coming with you. I need to find Gayle," Darius said, looking up at the castle in the distance.

CHAPTER 12

HILL OF RUIN

It didn't take them long to make their way back through the sewers. They left the stretcher leaning against the wall in the tunnel, and then made their way back to Aswin's basement in half the time.

They slipped back into the basement, checking on Judith as they did. She was sleeping with Kiera in the rough bed next to her.

"Man, what I wouldn't do for some sleep," Aswin whispered, wishing he could fall into his bed for a few hours, but dawn was coming, and he needed to get to the castle.

He grabbed his Dragon Keeper's bag from where he had left it. "Sam, stay here. If any guards show up, tell them I went to the caves. They might just arrest you. Don't fight them, Sam. Just do what they want you to do, you got it? You've got to protect your mother and wife. Don't go being a hero."

"Okay," Sam said in a small voice, not sure he was up for the task. He had never been a brave man, but maybe he could find it in him now.

They crept through the town's back alleys. The alleys were lined with trash, and rats scurried out of their way. Grand Avenue was heavily patrolled, and soldiers with torches went by every few minutes, but the soldiers weren't smart enough to realize that if someone wanted to avoid them, they could just duck down the back.

"Man, I'm already missing my staff," Darius said as he tripped on a pothole in the alley. He nearly went flying.

Aswin looked at him curiously. "Yeah, it's got to feel like a part of you is missing."

They arrived at the river, and Aswin started crossing, jumping across the stones.

"This takes me down memory lane," Darius chuckled, making his way across the stones. His feet still remembered, after all these years. His father used to take him and Aswin up to the dragon caves when they were little. "Ah, the path is still here and still treacherous. You want an old man to climb up that? With no light?"

"I do it every morning. Come on, Darius, stop being a crybaby. I'm older than you," Aswin grumbled. "It's not even that steep. If you remember, it looks worse than it is."

"Fine, fine." Darius said, shaking his head. This obviously was going to be the only way.

Aswin looked over his shoulder to the east. "It's almost time for daybreak. I don't see any dragons; this doesn't bode well." In fact, the dark shape of a nightfall dragon passed overhead, swooping into the main entrance higher up.

They climbed faster and then reached the main entrance, huffing and out of breath. Aswin was starting to feel his exhaustion creeping in. He had a headache, and his limbs felt heavy.

"Dragon Keeper. We were wondering when you would show up. And you brought Gayle's boy toy with you. How wonderful." A voice spoke from the cave entrance, and the dragon form of Linnea slipped out of the darkness.

"Linnea. I came here to take care of my dragons. If you've hurt them . . ." Aswin threatened, pointing at her.

She laughed. "We have quashed the spirit out of them, and a few died who resisted."

Aswin pushed past her into the main entrance and gasped when he saw the bodies of dragons littered across the floor. Five at least, and his heart broke when he saw Dahlia's corpse laying there, lifeless on the floor, her blood spilled around her.

He started crying and then looked at the other bodies. All were drakaina and had probably come to Dahlia's aide. He then noticed forms of dragons, dark purple and icy blues, all looking at him with their glowing eyes. Lacking nests here of their own, they had just sat to rest in the open area.

From the main hallway, Gayle came rushing out, followed by Doyle. She made her way to Darius and hugged him tightly. "Thora has awoken in Fresthav, and she's angry we left without her. We will leave shortly," she whispered in his ear.

"Good of you to show up, Aswin. We've been doing all your work for you. We took care of most of the injuries, but you'll need to follow up with some of them. Nasty bites, and we ran out of the liquor we found in your cabinet," Kai said, his purple form slithering forward.

"Thank you. I had other pressing matters to take care of."

"We didn't know what to do with the bodies, and the remaining sunrise dragons are so terrified, they won't talk to us or come out of their nests. They barely let us take care of their wounded, and some warriors wouldn't let us come into their nests," Linnea said, stamping her foot in frustration.

"Where is Torrid?" Aswin asked, looking at the bodies. He would have expected the fierce warrior to be leading the charge, especially after his daughter fell.

"We know of no Torrid," Gayle said. "Is he one of the warriors?"

"Yes, you would know Torrid. He's about twice as big as any other dragon here, with a tempter to boot," Aswin added.

"No, we haven't any dragon here like that," Doyle said.

"I'm going to start my rounds. I'll convince the sunrise dragons they can come collect the dead and move them to the crypts," Aswin said, looking around sadly. "I don't know where Nick is, but we need dragons to come greet the sun. It's waiting in the east, and it's already past sunrise."

"There will be no sunrise today," King Ibis slithered forward, his dark body sliding over the stone floor with a scrape.

"There has to be a sunrise, Ibis," Aswin said, looking at him coldly.

"No, there doesn't. We nightfall dragons have decided that since Nick is hiding upstairs, and won't show himself, we won't let the sunrise dragons fly. I think the little princeling is afraid of us."

"I can go get him if you would like. Now that Aswin is here, maybe he'll come down," Doyle offered, moving to the stairs.

"Yes, do that, Doyle. I would love to talk to King Nick now that we have fulfilled our end of the bargain," Ibis said, his yellow eyes burning.

Aswin brushed past him, heading down the hallway to tend to his dragons.

He was in Apple's nest, looking at a gash in his side. He had a small flask of alcohol in his bag, so he used it sparingly.

"I wouldn't let those other Dragon Keepers in. I don't trust them," Apple said, closing his eyes against the pain.

"I understand. We need to take care of the dead, Apple. I don't know where Torrid is, but Dahlia has fallen, along with a few others. Torrid would want his daughter in their crypt," Aswin said.

"I know. We will gather soon. We are all waiting for King Nick to make an appearance down here. He hasn't come down yet, and we don't know why."

"He can't change back into a human if he turns into a dragon. That's why," Aswin said, a lightbulb going off in his head. He started laughing. "Imagine, planning a coup, and then getting stuck as a human. It's quite delightful, really."

Aswin finished up with Apple, and then moved down to the

Chuvash nest. He peeked in and saw Sadie laying in her nest, her orange glowing eyes peeled on the entrance.

"Dragon Keeper. You have arrived," she smirked. "I have good news. My egg has started to hatch!"

"Really? I guess that's about right." Aswin hurried forward and looked at the bronze egg. A small crack ran across the top of it.

"How much longer?" she asked, looking at him closely.

"A few days. Probably three. By the end of the week, this little one will be here," Aswin said, running his hand over the shell. It was warm, as it should be, and he could feel life quivering inside, aching to get out.

"My son, the Crown Prince of Dumara," Sadie said, a dreamy look coming over her eyes.

Aswin thought of the egg, hidden in his wooden box, and he avoided looking at her, for fear his face would show his disgust.

"What, Dragon Keeper? Are you unhappy with that? My husband is King, and Dahlia is dead, and her egg is lost. We can't find it, but without the mother to keep it warm, it is dead."

"True, eggs must be kept warm," Aswin said, nodding. The spot behind the woodstove was perfect.

"Nick hasn't been down yet," she said unhappily, "Because you weren't here. Now that you have returned, Aswin, things will be right again."

He nodded, not bothering to explain that he was here to take care of the dragons, and not Nick. Even if he died for his rebellion, he wouldn't do anything for that man.

He finished with her and then moved on down through the caves. He was tending to a burn on the dragon known as Ace when Darius hurried in. "Aswin, Torrid is here, and there is a bit of a problem."

"Oh dear. I'm coming," Aswin said, grabbing his bag and nearly tripping as he hurried out of the nest.

"I'm coming, too," Apple said, slipping out of his nest, grimacing at the pain. He roared for the rest of the warriors when he got to the hall, and they appeared from their nests, joining him as they silently and dangerously slipped down the hall.

————

Torrid stood at the entrance, saying nothing, looking over the dead bodies of his clan mates impassively. His eyes rested on his daughter, and inside, his heart broke into a thousand pieces. First, he lost his wife, and now his only daughter. But he didn't let it show on his face. He heard the rumble from down the hallway and recognized the roar of Apple, one of his warriors.

The nightfall and winter dragons were alerted and rose from their slumber.

Behind him, the sun was rising, an hour late, but there. He had greeted the sun and brought it with him from Terrek. He had to stop last night, near Cypress Lake, and sleep, as he was too exhausted from his round trip. He had expected to meet his clan mates this morning, halfway home, but when no one had arrived to greet the sun, he had realized that something was wrong, so he had greeted the sun himself.

Now he understood why. He had seen the nightfall dragons arriving and understood now what had happened. They, along with the winter dragons, had pierced the inner sanctuary of their clan caves, and this was the result.

Torrid's throat burned with grief as his friends filed in, and he saw their spirits were crushed. No one would look him in the eye, and they slunk to his side, avoiding the winter and nightfall dragons who had conquered them.

Aswin made his way through the crowd and approached him. "Torrid. I'm sorry. Your daughter was dead when I arrived."

"She fought against us. She was ferocious. It took five of us to take her," Linnea said, looking at him closely and moving forward toward him. Her drakainas fell in beside her, and they approached the massive warrior as one.

He still said nothing. "Where is Nick? He must answer for this," he finally hissed.

"I am here!" A voice roared from the stairs, and Nick changed and walked out to them. He was surrounded by a hundred of the castle soldiers, who stood with their mouths open, looking at the mass of dragons of all colors before them. They had never seen so many dragons gathered.

Nick's body shimmered as it shifted to his dragon form. He stood, filling the entrance, looking mighty with his front legs spread, and his chest puffed out. The soldiers gasped and nearly dropped their swords. The secret revealed, none of them believed it.

Torrid laughed. It was a chuckle at first, and then it shook his whole body until the tears came. And once they started as tears of mirth, they soon changed to tears of grief.

"Why are you laughing?" Nick demanded, his red scales catching the light as he moved forward, stepping around the fallen bodies of his dragons. His soldiers stood frozen, not understanding anything that was happening, but understanding something momentous was taking place.

"You. You think you have won; you think you have taken the throne from your father, but it takes more than a bit of poison to win the throne. You also have to win the hearts of your people, and you have failed in that respect miserably."

"I am your King!" Nick roared. "You will respect me, or I will crush you!" The soldiers behind him flinched at the roars. They pushed back toward the stairs. They all wished to flee this madness, but they feared even more the anger of this Dragon King before them.

Sumac and the rest of Nick's die-hard supporters slunk out of the caves, surrounding their King with evil smirks.

"We will care for our dead. I must move my daughter to our crypt, and we must move the others. Who will join me?" Torrid looked around, and one by one, dragons moved to the sides of the fallen drakainas.

He moved over to take one of his daughters' legs, and together, his warriors joined him, pulling the massive bodies down the hallways to the crypts. It would take them hours to complete this task. This would give him time to conspire with his warriors, deep in the heart of the caves, where no nightfall or winter dragon would dare follow, because places of death were sacred, and even they could respect that.

"I should go with them," Darius said, following. "I can say the death rites of the Dragon God, even if I no longer have my staff to bless the bodies."

"NO!" Nick roared. "You will stay here with your brother. Aswin, you are my Dragon Keeper now. And where is Mila? One of you will be bound to me."

"You will not find Mila. She has fled the city, safe from you. And I will not serve you! I will not serve the man who killed my friend. I serve only my dragons," Aswin said, spitting in his direction.

"I'm sure I can persuade you, Dragon Keeper," he said, striding forward to Darius. He picked him up with one claw, tightening his grip. Darius squeezed his eyes shut. Nick brought the man to his face, so close Darius could feel his hot dragon breath. "I've never tried human before, but I suppose he would make a tasty little mouth full."

"Please! Don't kill him." Gayle stepped forward unexpectedly. "I beg of you, King Nick."

"What do you want?" Aswin said, his voice dangerous.

"Give me an astragenica potion," he demanded.

"I will not. Eat my brother if you have to, then there will be no one to bind you," Aswin said, his eyes narrowing.

Nick paused, considering the sorcerer in his hand. His tongue flicked out, touching Darius' face. He didn't taste very good, and Aswin, damn him, had a point. He could bind someone else as his Dragon Keeper if Aswin wouldn't cooperate.

"Please, King Nick. You can have one of my astragenica potions. I brought a bunch," Gayle said, fishing one out of her bag and holding it up.

"Give it to me," he demanded, opening his mouth.

She hurried forward and poured it into his mouth. He quickly put Darius down and changed back into human form.

They all stared at him, completely naked, standing before them. He felt their judgment and turned his head toward one of his soldiers. The awkward beat passed. "You, bring me my clothes. The rest of you, close your mouths and seize the Fletcher brothers. Throw them in my dungeon, and I'll deal with them later."

"No! He will come back to Fresthav with me!" Gayle said, moving in front of Darius. He smiled and leaned down and gave her a kiss.

"I think I'm going to have to stay here, dear. But thank you. I appreciate you saving my bacon when my OWN brother apparently doesn't care if I get eaten by a psychotic dragon."

"I care, Darius. I was calling his bluff," Aswin argued as he watched the soldiers advance toward them. The sunrise dragons around them started mumbling in disagreement, realizing their beloved Dragon Keeper was going to be arrested.

"Please, take this vile man away. He's been nothing but a distraction to my Dragon Keeper, and my mother demands our return soon. We will be leaving here soon, Nick," Linnea said firmly, stepping forward. "I think our work here is done."

The soldiers reached Aswin and grabbed him roughly. They snatched his bag away, and it was delivered to Nick.

They more hesitantly approached Darius, who stood glaring at them, his arms crossed. If he had his staff, he could blast them all out the entrance of the cave, but then again, he would probably soon thereafter end up as a dragon snack, so maybe that wasn't the best idea. One man against a crowd of angry dragons didn't seem like good odds.

He held up his empty hands and allowed them to grab him. Soon, both Aswin and he were standing in front of Nick, who was smirking. "Take them to the dungeon and hang them from the ceiling. A few hours of that will loosen them up a bit, make them more willing to work with me."

Nick turned to the remaining sunrise dragons. "Thank you to my supporters. I know this has been a difficult time. I mourn the deaths of our brethren with you, but we will rise stronger than ever, with our new partners, the nightfall and winter dragons. We can look forward to peace and unity with our new brothers. And today I announce the betrothal of my son, soon to be born, and the daughter of Linnea and Kai. Light, fire, ice, and night. Their powerful union will unite the four kingdoms."

A cheer went up from Sumac and his friends, as Aswin and Darius were shoved toward the stairs. There was silence from the rest of the sunrise dragons. Gayle stood crying in the back.

Prince Kai stepped forward with Linnea, under the gaze of his father, King Ibis. "We also announce that we have decided formally to take each other as mates. I will live in Fresthav with my Queen, to raise our daughter and future daughters together."

"Maybe I'll consent to a son, just for you, my love," she said, smiling and showing her teeth.

———

Torrid and the rest of his warriors finished with their grim task, gently lowering Dahlia into the crypt of her ancestors. Torrid watched her body slip into the hole to lie next to his beloved mate, his face wet with tears.

The other bodies around them, one by one, were lowered into their family crypts. On the way down here, and out of the hearing of others, Torrid revealed that Alex was still alive.

"Aswin has hidden him somewhere. The true King still breathes."

They whispered amongst themselves, wondering where Aswin had hidden Alex. They surmised that Mila must be with him, tucked away in some secret hiding place in the city. That must have been where Aswin had been all day yesterday, when the city was burning and dragons were dying.

The warriors of the sunrise clans were beaten and depressed, but hope still flickered.

"We should pay our respects to King Rand while we are down here," Torrid said, and he joined the warriors at the edge of the Chuvash crypt. They looked down into the pit below, seeing the nearly completely decomposed dragon body of Cassandra, and next to her, King Rand, bloated and dead. The sheet had slipped off him, and they could see him lying next to his wife. "It's a shame we can't fly to send him on to the Dragon God," May, a magenta dragon, said, his eyes filled with sadness.

"Look, there is only one body. Where is King Alex? Where is he? It's true then, he still lives!" the warriors said, hope rising. They hadn't quite believed Torrid at first, but now they saw with their own eyes.

"Warriors, I have a plan. Come, gather with me. I will tell you before we return to the upper floors. To make this work, we will have to slip out with no words, but King Dayia of Terrek has promised any sunrise dragon who wants it, sanctuary."

They all started discussing what that meant, and how they could escape. They would keep fighting and support Alex, until he could return to take his rightful throne.

———

One by one, the warriors loyal to Alex slipped to the entrance and into the skies, avoiding looking at the nightfall and winter dragons who lingered. A squad of soldiers remained, lounging against the walls of the hallways, trying to stay out of the way of the dragons. They all looked terrified.

It wasn't until they were nearly all gone, when Ibis noticed Torrid, the huge butter colored dragon, heading for the entrance.

"Hey, you! You're that huge dragon. Where are you going?" he demanded, stepping in front of him.

Torrid stopped. "If you will pardon me, I just interred my daughter. My heart is heavy."

Ibis looked at him with suspicious eyes and then looked around.

"Where are all the dragons you left with? There were a bunch of them. You left as a group."

"What does it matter to you? I'm headed to escort my daughter's spirit home to the Dragon God. Do you have such a tradition?"

"We do," Ibis said, nodding.

"Well then, let me pass!" Torrid demanded, stepping to the right. Ibis made no move to stop him. He felt for the dragon.

Sumac was loitering around, trying to make nice with the other dragons. They all ignored him or told him to move along. He saw Torrid heading to the entrance. "Hey! They've all left! All the warriors have left! I just realized!"

"Goodbye, Sumac. Until we meet again, and I can repay you for your treachery. Tell Nick I will return, and we will place the true King back on his throne," Torrid said, hissing in Sumac's direction as he launched into the afternoon.

Sumac made to give chase, but as soon as he got to the edge, he saw Torrid rapidly flying eastward, beating his massive yellow wings faster than Sumac could even dream of flying. He spotted a group of dragons, some twenty strong, circling in the far distance, waiting for Torrid to join them. He sighed, realizing he would never catch Torrid, and even if he did, what would he do? Torrid or any one of the others would beat him out of the sky with one swipe.

Sumac turned, as he saw his King standing behind him. "How many of the warriors left with him?" Nick said. He was in his human form but had paid a visit to Sadie and the egg, marveling that his son would hatch soon.

"All of them, Your Majesty," Sumac said, looking off into the distance.

"I can't believe you let them escape. And what was that line about the true King? Do you think they know where Dahlia's egg went?"

"Maybe. Maybe they snuck it out somehow or hid it in the caves."

"Perhaps. Perhaps it's time to visit the Dragon Keeper and the sorcerer and find out what they know. Guards!" Nick yelled, and the squad of guards who had remained jumped to attention. "Search the nests. You are looking for a gold and red egg. If you find any, note what nest they are in, I'll investigate later." He recalled Dahlia's egg was gold, with red streaks. A unique egg, and one he could identify by sight.

"Yes, Your Majesty." His Captain stood at attention and gave him a salute, hoping that the dragons would be amicable to them peeking around their nests. He somehow had a feeling they would not be so happy with this prospect.

———

Torrid and his warriors turned toward the east. He would send Dahlia's spirit off to the Dragon God. He wished he could send Rand's also, but his son would have to do that, and he doubted Nick even cared.

He roared, and the surrounding dragons joined him, their rays of light shooting straight into the sun. He felt Dahlia's spirit join his, and it was sad, but tinged with hope. He turned his eyes on her specter, and she nodded at him, unable to speak, but glad her father was at her side for the last time.

———

Her last blessing, before she slipped into the majestic beyond, was sent toward her egg. She could sense that it was safe, and that made her happy. She caught sight of her mother waiting for her, and just beside her was the Dragon God, awesome and divine. She spread her spectral spirit wings wide and took one last glance at her father, who nodded. "Farewell, my dear, you were brave and fought well. You have made me proud."

She roared for one last time, and her light joined the light of the afterlife, and her shade faded from this earth.

Chapter 13

Brothers

Aswin hung from the ceiling in the middle of the room, his wrists bound and then slipped over a hook for just this torturous purpose. His feet were inches from the floor. He had been here for hours, and he was in immense pain, but he endured. He wondered how long Nick would leave him here, and if he would die on this hook, or if someone would come to cut him down before his joints wrenched from their sockets.

Besides him, Darius hung in the same manner. He had been moaning in pain for what seemed hours, but now he just hung, his chin resting on his chest, his eyes closed.

He had passed the dungeons on his way down to the Dragon Caves thousands of times, but he had never given them much thought. Sometimes they would hear laughter or screams, or the prisoners would peer out at them, or try to grab them.

The dungeon was one long room, with one small window at one end, and the heavy iron door on the other. There were no cells, just rings on the walls, where prisoners were shackled.

Right now, there were a half dozen other men, shackled to the walls by thick manacles and chains. Some appeared to have been here for years, if not decades, their long hair matted, and their bodies skeletal. Those sad men hunched near the wall, whimpering, and muttering to themselves.

A few of the men looked like new arrivals, strong, healthy, with bright eyes. Unfortunately, they were all out of reach, and none could help them with their suffering.

One man, a man with a thick chest, a brown beard, and a low voice, was shackled closest to them. "It's the Dragon Keeper, and the sorcerer," he said to the others.

Darius twisted his head around so he could look at the man. "I'm Darius Fletcher, this is my brother, Aswin. We are kind of in a spot, as you can see."

"My name is Miles. I got caught up in that rioting yesterday and got knocked unconscious by a city guard," he said, touching his forehead, where a large bloody lump was clear.

"Nice to meet you, Miles," Aswin said softly as his shoulders screamed in pain.

———

Time passed, and they cried, screamed, moaned, passed out, and cursed Nick up one side and down the other.

Miles sat with his back to the wall, looking at the brothers sadly. He wished he could help.

The other men around them talked softly. They had all been caught up in the rioting yesterday. They were men from the docks, fishermen, sailors, stevedores. They all believed Nick had killed their King, and they had picked up whatever weapons they had in protest.

Unfortunately, they had ended up in the crowd of people who wanted to loot, kill, and burn the city of Dumara. The thieves, cutthroats, and opportunists of Dumara, who only wanted profit from this moment of uncertainty.

Miles was with the mob that had broken into the tailor's shop. He saw the madmen kill Franklin Wright, beating him with clubs and bricks. He had turned and thrown up when they finally killed him with this own sword. Miles had frequented the tailor's shop before, and had flirted with the daughter.

He realized this was not for him. He had turned away just as they found the tailor's wife; he heard her screams and stumbled into the alleyway to get sick again, and he had tried to get as far away as possible.

He had intended to return home, to his little flop house by the docks, when a group of ruffians had found him in the alley. The beat him within an inch of his life, stealing the few coins he had in his pocket, and had left him for dead. It wasn't until the morning, when the wagons had rolled through the city with squads of soldiers, that he had been picked up.

They had thought him dead at first, kicking him with a sharp boot in his side. He had moaned, and sat up, only to be roughly cuffed and thrown in the back of the wagon with the other men before him.

He did not know what his charges were, but he was innocent. Well, maybe not completely innocent. He had marched with the riots and thrown stones and broken windows. But he hadn't hurt anyone, and he certainly hadn't assaulted decent, law-abiding citizens.

He shook his head, recognizing he was in a precarious position. He wondered what his charges would be. He couldn't afford a lawyer, so he would have to represent himself. With King Rand dead, who knew if he would even get a fair trial?

Miles heard steps on the stairs and the sound of voices. It was getting dark, and the Fletcher brothers had been quiet for some time. He wondered if they were still alive; they had stopped crying a while ago.

The door flew open, and soldiers came in, placing torches throughout the room. One carried a basket and started handing out chunks of bread. Behind them strode in Nick, wearing his father's robe, and the crown on his head. Miles wanted to laugh. He looked like a little pretend king, but he held it back. He had no desire to die today.

Nick walked over to Aswin and looked at him with a sadistic little grin on his face. "Have you had enough, Dragon Keeper? Will you consent to be bound to me?"

Aswin lifted his chin, staring at Nick with hatred in his eyes. "I will never be your Dragon Keeper. Kill me."

Nick shook his head and then turned to Darius. "Your girlfriend left earlier, with the rest of the winter dragons. I don't think she wanted to leave you here. She was crying. Linnea was quite forceful though."

Darius nodded. "Gayle knows I'll come for her."

Nick laughed. "Well, that's going to be hard to do, seeing as you're tied up, hanging from my ceiling."

"It's not been a great time; I'll give you that. Your guest accommodations could be improved," Darius said, with just a twinkle of mirth in his eyes. He really was in too much pain to be his usually snippy self.

"Can you bind me to Aswin, even if he doesn't consent?" Nick said, moving closer to Darius, so close that he could feel Nick's hot breath on his face.

"I couldn't even if I wanted to. I don't have my staff of power," Darius said, a small smile touching his lips.

"What do you mean!" Nick roared, looking around. The sorcerer always carried that bloody staff. He had never seen the man without it.

"I lost it. Or rather, it broke in all the commotion. No staff, no magic power."

"Cut them down," Nick demanded, and a soldier drew out a dagger and sawed Aswin's hands free. He dropped to the ground, his feet hitting the ground first, and then stumbling forward. He sobbed as Darius dropped next to him. The brothers sat back-to-back, their heads down.

The soldiers attached a shackle to their ankles and drug them over to the wall, securing them both in the same loop of chain. "What have you done with Dahlia's egg, Aswin? I know you hid it somewhere. My men have searched the caves from top to bottom.

It must be kept warm, and we found it in no nest. Where did you hide it?"

Aswin looked up, and a smile came to his lips. "You'll never find it."

Nick sighed and nodded to his men. They descended on Aswin and started kicking and punching him. After a few minutes, they stopped and stepped back.

"Let's try this again. Where is your daughter? She can be my Dragon Keeper if you won't."

Aswin smiled again. "You won't find her, either. Do you think I'm stupid, Nick? Why would I let Mila wander around town? I know who you are."

"You try me, Dragon Keeper. Tell me why I should keep you alive if you won't help me? Your brother won't help me. I should hang both of you here, with these other traitors, and put your head on the gates."

"You can't kill us. For one, I'm the only one here who knows the recipes for all the potions. Even if you do find another Dragon Keeper, they aren't going to know how to make anything. And I didn't say I wouldn't be THE Dragon Keeper. I just won't be YOUR Dragon Keeper. If any of the dragons in the caves get sick or injured, I would be happy to help them. Just not you, you murdering toad. I can't believe you killed your father to take his throne. Blood is on your hands, Nick. The blood of your father, and your people. They hate you. You are the King of Dumara in name only. You will never win their hearts."

"You will cooperate, or you will rot here forever. It's your choice," Nick said, turning on his heel. "But it looks like I need a new Dragon Keeper, regardless. What was the name of your shopkeeper? I bet he knows a thing or two."

"Sam," Aswin said, "And he already knows you are coming."

———

Later, after the blood flow had returned to their hands, they picked up their stale bread from where it had fallen on the ground.

"I can't feel my fingertips, Aswin. Do you think this is permanent? My wrists don't seem to work right, either."

"Maybe. My shoulder feels like it's torn or something." Aswin said, shifting in the dark. The brothers were still back-to-back, and they had dozed off in the darkness.

Miles spoke up. The man was on the wall next to them. "Those were some brave words. I don't know if I would have been able to tell the King to go stuff it like you two did."

"I've known Nick since he was a dragonling. He is full of anger, he's always been jealous of his brother and father, and now the throne is his. He will stop at nothing, but he knows I'm right. He's in between a rock and a hard place," Aswin said. He could just make out the face of Miles in the faint light.

"Did you hear him say he was going to hang us?" Miles said, his voice full of fear. A few voices rose in agreement in the darkness.

"I did. He will make a big show of it, though." Aswin tore at the hard bread with his teeth. He was famished, and this was the first thing he had to eat all day.

"Is it true King Nick is a dragon? The men and I were talking while you were asleep. We heard the guards at the door arguing about it. They said they saw him change with their own eyes," Miles said, his voice lowering.

"Yes. It's true," Darius said. "He didn't keep that secret long, did he? Hundreds of years of his grandfathers, protecting the secret at all costs, and the first thing he does is shape-shift in front of a squad of soldiers. I guarantee the entire city knows by tomorrow morning."

"So, the stories of the Dragon God are true?" Miles said, his eyes full of wonder.

"Well, more or less," Darius admitted. "I'm the sorcerer, and I bestow the blessing of the Dragon God. He gave the sorcerer the power a long time ago, but I sadly seem to have lost my staff."

"You could bust us out of here with a staff?" Miles asked. "I heard about the wedding last year. That was you, wasn't it?"

"Yeah, but I promise, I had nothing to do with that earthquake. That was all the Dragon God. I wouldn't want to be Nick when the Dragon God cometh."

"What?" Miles asked, tilting his head.

"What drumbeat are we on, Aswin?"

"Three, the last time I checked," Aswin said with a sigh, crossing his arms across his chest to keep warm.

"Well, we are running out of time. In the Book of the Dragon God, he talks about his second coming. At five beats, he will return. It's not looking good," Darius said with a frown.

"What happens when he shows back up?"

"Death, destruction, the end of life as we know it," Darius said, looking out the little window to the darkness outside. He wondered how much time they had left. It could be six months, or a decade. Only the Dragon God knew how fast the sands of time slipped by.

———

Down in the city, Sam awoke. He had been sleeping on a chair in the store's front, holding on to a broom. He heard the chirping of birds first and saw the sun rising from the east.

He didn't know what time it was, but Kiera came up from the basement. "Mother seems better today. I came up to fix her some tea and find some porridge for breakfast."

Sam got up and moved across the room to her. He gently gathered his wife in his arms. "I love you, Kiera," he said, squeezing her tight. It had taken that riot yesterday, and her by his side to finally realize it was Kiera he loved with all his heart and soul. The final piece of his heart, that he had held out for Mila, slipped into place.

"What's all this about?" she laughed as she gave him a kiss. "Come upstairs with me. This mess can wait."

They walked up the stairs, and Sam sat at the table while Kiera bustled around. He looked around the room, his eyes settling on the woodpile behind the stove.

"Was the fire out this morning?" he asked, moving behind the now blazing stove.

"Not completely. We lit it last night to make tea, remember? There were still some glowing embers, and the stove top was still warm."

"Kiera, make sure this fire doesn't go out," he said, looking at the wood box behind it. He moved a piece of wood and touched the egg, streaked with red, and felt it was still warm. Good.

He did some quick math and then looked at his wife. "Our child is due in July."

"Yes, toward the end," Kiera said, a smile crossing her face. "Do you think we will stay here, or move back into my mother's place, as soon as we get it cleaned up?"

"We will stay here. We must look after this egg. It will hatch around the same time our child will be born."

"How can we hide a dragonling?" Kiera asked, looking over at the egg.

"I do not know. We will figure it out."

"We will have to ask Aswin. Maybe he has an idea," Kiera said, pulling the steaming kettle off the stovetop. She gave the porridge a few quick stirs and ladled up a bowl to take to her mother.

Sam grabbed the teapot and poured out three mugs. "I do not know when Aswin will return." Sam said, looking around. "We will take his room for now, and your mother can have Mila's."

Kiera hurried down to deliver her mother the breakfast. When she didn't return right away and he heard angry voices downstairs, he hurried down.

"Where is Sam Arbuckle?" a soldier demanded from the doorway. Kiera was glaring at him.

"I am Sam. I'm the shopkeeper here. This is my wife, Kiera. What seems to be the problem?" he said, stepping forward in front of his wife.

The soldier stepped aside, and with horror, Sam saw Nick Chuvash behind him.

"Sam Arbuckle, we need to talk. You have something I want," Nick said, grinning.

Sam felt panic rise in his chest. He knew, they knew, he had the egg. "Oh yeah? What would that be?"

"Knowledge, Sam. I want your knowledge. Come with me."

"Your Majesty, this is not a good time. My shop is destroyed, the windows are gaping open, my father-in-law lays dead across the street. We need to collect his body today and make preparations for the funeral. My mother-in-law is grievously wounded, she's in the basement, resting."

"Why the basement?" Nick asked, looking over the Dragon Keeper's shop. It was destroyed. It would take a lot of work to reopen.

"The place has been looted. We will move her back upstairs, but that is wrecked also. We need to buy some new feather mattresses. But my mother-in-law is resting comfortably, I assure you."

Nick pointed to two of his men. "Stay here, and help the shopkeeper's wife. Clean up this front room, collect her father's body, and board up the windows. You, come with me," he ordered, pointing at Sam.

"Yes, sir," Sam said, throwing a look at Kiera. She nodded; she would make sure the soldiers stayed out of the upstairs apartments.

Sam stepped out of the building and followed Nick and the guards up to the castle. He didn't feel like he had much of a choice.

———

They arrived at the castle and marched right through the gates. The soldiers at the front approached Nick. "Your Majesty, we continue our patrols of the city. We are focusing on the dock area, and we have raided several bars where the unsavory hang out. Unfortunately, we have no more leads on who led the riots. It seems to have just arisen, naturally. Desperate men taking advantage of the change of power."

"Fine, focus on the market district and the highlands neighborhood. Our citizens will appreciate the increased patrols until some of the damage can be repaired."

"What of the men we picked up yesterday? Are we giving them a trial?" the guard asked. "The dungeon is full now. We should clear them out. Less work for us if we do."

"We will hold formal trials in one week's time. They will hang for their crimes. All of them," Nick said firmly.

"Excuse me, sir, you aren't going to hang Aswin Fletcher, are you?" Sam said, panic-stricken.

"That remains to be seen, Sam Arbuckle. Come with me." Nick strode into the palace, and Sam followed. The few times he had accompanied Aswin to the dragon caves, they had come from the river path. He had never been in the castle, and he looked around at the opulence that surrounded him.

Growing up as the son of a poor, alcoholic, retired soldier, he had never imagined people lived like this. This front hallway was as large as his childhood home, and the elaborately carved side table was probably worth more than the humble house his parents still lived in, if you wanted to call their wretched existence living. When he could, he brought his mother groceries. He never gave them cash because his father just drank it all away. Morris Arbuckle received a monthly stipend from the crown for his military service, but it disappeared into the bottle every month.

He followed dutifully, trying to avoid staring at the wall hangings, art, and crystal chandeliers that lined the walls. Soon, they arrived at a simple door set in the hallway. Nick opened it, and they all shuffled inside, moving down and down into the darkness. It was a circular stairway, and he found himself turned around. He knew the dragon caves were somewhere below him.

They stopped at a heavy iron door, and a soldier fumbled around for the key. Finally, it was opened, and they all stepped inside.

Sam could make out prisoners chained to the wall. They all looked up at him with hopeless eyes.

Nick turned on him, pulled out a dagger, and he was seized from behind by a guard. "What is the meaning of this?" Sam said, trying to stay calm and not to struggle.

"Oh, Aswin! Oh, Darius! You have a visitor," Nick said, practically giggling.

"Sam. Just do what he says," Aswin said, looking up from the floor where he was shackled.

"Of course. Your Majesty, what do you want me to do?" Sam said, trying to keep his throat as far away from the dagger point as possible.

"I want you to be my Dragon Keeper," Nick said, looking him over. "Aswin won't do it."

"I will, sir. I'll be your Dragon Keeper. The only problem is, I'm not fully trained," Sam said, not liking how desperate his voice sounded.

"And why aren't you fully trained, Sam? I'm disappointed." Nick pulled the knife away and started to play with it, staring at Sam angrily.

"I'm just the shopkeeper, sir. I make the basic potions. Astragenica, healing balm, and the soothing potions that the housewives like. I tend to the till and stock the shelves. I've come up to the cave a few times with Aswin, but he has always directed me."

Nick turned to Aswin. "Let's make a deal, shall we? You tell this boy what he needs to know when he needs to know it, and I'll let you and your brother live."

Aswin nodded, not looking Nick in the eye.

"And if you decide not to cooperate, then I'll just have to kill all three of you," Nick hissed.

"Sir! I have a wife, and our first child is on the way!" Sam said, fear rising in his voice.

"Well, you are going to have to work hard for me. I expect you here every morning, to deliver an astragenica potion to my wife, Sadie, and I. Our son will be born any minute now, and I expect you to make sure he's healthy. Do you understand, Sam Arbuckle?" Nick said.

"Yes, sir. I will be happy to be here, as much as you need me. But I know nothing about dragonlings. I need to consult with Aswin," Sam said.

"I'll let you have access to the dungeon, then. There will be two men at the door from now on. They will let you in, of course, after searching you. Come and go as you please."

"Thank you, Your Majesty," Sam said, feeling overwhelmed. He couldn't fill Aswin's shoes, but apparently, he would be expected to.

"I took his bag from him earlier. Maybe you could use it. I'll return it to you. Now, if you will excuse me, I'll leave you to discuss your options. I must shift to my dragon form and visit my wife and check on our egg. Please stop to change me back before you leave," Nick left, happy that he could now change back and forth between his dragon and human form. He hadn't expected this being such a problem, or he might have made sure Mila was in his custody before all this went down. She had slipped out of his fingers though, and probably Alex's egg with her.

———

After Nick had left, and the soldiers had retreated to the door, Aswin sighed. "Come closer, Sam, so the soldiers don't overhear us."

Sam hurried and dropped to one knee near his mentor. He wanted to cry when he looked at Aswin. He was battered and bruised, with one eye blackened and swollen shut. Darius looked little better.

"Be glad I broke my staff. Now Nick couldn't force me to bind you to him. You don't want to be in his mind," Darius said, grinning.

"But I won't be able to speak to dragons," Sam said, "Isn't that going to be a problem?"

"Yes, you'll have to take notes, and then come to me. I can probably tell you what's wrong just by a description," Aswin said.

"How do I look over Nick's dragonling? What am I looking for?" Sam asked. It seemed like that would be one of his first tasks.

"You want to make sure the dragonling is active and moving around. His eyes are clear, and his breathing is strong. He should be full of energy right away. If he's lethargic or if he can't stand, then we have a problem. You may need to administer a vitality potion."

"I don't know how to make one of those," Sam said, his forehead wrinkling.

"No worries. We don't use them very often, and they are very easy to make. Goldenrod, molasses, ginger, and root of the salacious plant," Aswin said, rattling off the instructions from memory.

"I'm going to have to bring parchment and a pencil, so I can take notes. I think this is going to be impossible."

"Sam, just do what he says, okay? We will help you. You'll be our man on the outside. I know Aswin still has a fortune in banknotes. Use what you need," Darius said, and Aswin glared at him, but didn't argue.

CHAPTER 14

NEW NORMAL

Every day, Sam kissed his wife goodbye, checked on the dragon egg, and then headed through the newly rebuilt and restocked shop to the dragon caves. During the day, Kiera worked the till and helped customers.

One of the first things he had done was to find a barrister to represent Miles. No one had seen the man commit any crimes, and the very expensive lawyer had argued that Miles had simply been a victim himself, after being robbed, beaten, and left for dead. They had got him and several of his friends freed, and he had slipped back into the underground of Dumara, where he whispered to all who would listen that the Prince was still alive, and that the tyrant Nick had killed his father.

Few believed him, but some did, and a spirit of rebellion rose. The poor and displaced of Dumara resented their new King. Miles smiled, and continued to build the support, whispering that Alex was the true King, and he would do a much better job if he returned to the throne. Most agreed.

It didn't help that the secret of the dragons had been revealed. The soldiers had wasted no time in spreading the story that they had seen the King transform before their eyes, and now everyone viewed him instantly with suspicion.

Since they had buried Franklin Wright just two weeks earlier, the tailor shop had been boarded up. Judith was considering selling the location. "I don't know if I have the heart to return to that shop. Franklin and I built it, and every time I step through those doors, I relive the trauma of that day all over again."

Sam understood and gave her time and space. Besides, in a few months, his child would be born, and Judith had promised to look after the baby for them.

Sam walked the path that Aswin used to walk every day, thinking about what he would have to do that morning. He approached the caves and was greeted by Rose, who nudged him on the shoulder playfully. Although the drakaina couldn't speak to him, he knew he was liked. He spread the message that Aswin was in the dungeon, upstairs, and that he was only working temporarily, until the boss was released. He sensed a growing unhappiness with the sunrise dragons.

The nightfall dragons still lurked around, even taking nests in their caves. King Ibis of Murdad was seen often in the caves and in the castle halls.

He checked into the Chuvash nest, and the bronze baby dragonling, named Calvin, was lying on his back, looking up at his mother with big brown eyes.

"How's the boy doing today, Sadie?" he talked as he walked up the nest. He knew they listened to him, and he would have loved to hear what they had to say back. She blinked her eyes and lowered her head. He realized she had a deer by the side of the nest. She was tearing off strips, and lowering them to her son, who gulped them up hungrily.

Sam sighed and rubbed the dragonling's stomach. At only a few weeks old, he was just about four feet long. The baby wiggled under his hand, his little claws waving in the air. "Healthy as a horse, Sadie. Aswin said to keep feeding him well. That's the most important thing for a dragonling, lots of meat. Looks like you have that covered."

She lowered her head and looked at Sam eye-to-eye. She blinked once and nodded her head, then went back to her task.

Sam noticed a dragon slide in and gave a low grumble. Sadie slipped out of the nest, and the dark red drakaina took her spot.

He headed through the caves, checking on the older dragons. There had been no injuries lately, although there had been a few cases of dragon fever. He had covered his mouth and washed his hands as Aswin instructed.

He stopped in the main hall, and Sadie was waiting for him, her mouth held open impatiently. He didn't realize she wanted to change this morning. If he had been able to speak to her, she could have told him. "Sorry, Sadie, I didn't realize you were waiting for me," he said, giving her the potion. She changed, and then threw him an evil glance. "My clothes, you dullard," she hissed, tossing her dark hair and covering her chest with her hands.

"Oh, sorry," he stuttered, pivoting to the stores they kept here just for that purpose. He found what he was looking for, Sadie's long and elegant black velvet dress, and her golden cape, with the crest of Dumara on the back. She snatched it from his hands and quickly dressed.

Nick swooped in through the cave entrance, landing with a soft thump. Sumac and several of his close associates soon followed. Every day, Sam was right on time so the King couldn't complain that he was slacking on his duties. He delivered the potion and watched as Nick transformed in front of him. He handed him his fine clothes; the King had court today. Sadie must be joining him.

"Thank you, Sam," Nick said with a grin, clapping him on the back. "How are my dragons today? I trust you've already checked on them all?"

"Oh yes, sir. They are all quite fine. The dragons that had dragon fever have all recovered. Your son is healthy and growing."

"Come my dear, we have court today, and we have a special

guest from Terrek. I'm sure you will be fascinated to hear what he has to say today," Nick said, kissing her hand.

"Oh yes, I can't wait!" she exclaimed, throwing her head back and laughing.

"Can I get an extra astragenica potion today, Sam? I have a little demonstration I want to make for our diplomat."

"Of course, sir." Sam grabbed his Dragon Keeper bag and pulled out one of the astragenica potions. He would need to make another batch tonight when he got back home. Sadie took it from him and tucked it into the pocket of her dress. The royal couple turned and headed up the stairs.

He headed up the stairs behind them, planning to stop at the dungeon. He had some exciting news for the boss.

————

The royal couple had arrived a half an hour early. "I have a wonderful idea, Sadie," he whispered into her ear. He sat on his throne, and leaned over to kiss her neck.

She looked at him with a smile and then lifted her skirts. They had plenty of time before court started.

At the top of the hour exactly, the bailiff peaked his head in. He had heard suspicious noises coming from the throne room, but he dared not enter before it was time for court to begin.

The Queen and King had finished their task, and the King looked at his bailiff with a small smile on his face while tucking in his shirt. "I think we are ready to begin. Sadie, are you satisfied this morning?"

"Quite satisfied, my love," she said, adjusting her bodice. The bailiff looked back and forth between them and then turned on his heel and went to gather the first visitor of the morning.

"Lord Zeon Marx, Diplomat from the Kingdom of Terrek," the bailiff announced.

The lord swept in, wearing an emerald green doublet. He had a large, obnoxious hat, with a huge plume on the brim. He swept it off his head dramatically and bowed. "Your Majesty, it is an honor to come to you today. I bear tidings from King Cleon, your father-in-law."

"Really, it's been some time since we spoke to King Cleon. How long has it been, dear?" Nick said, glancing over at his wife. She sat idly examining her fingernails, and she covered her mouth with a yawn.

"Well, let's see. It was before our wedding, which my parents sadly did not attend. Huh, the last time we spoke to them together was at our engagement party. I seem to remember they weren't thrilled with our announcement."

"Oh yes, there was that. Although they held up their end of the bargain with my father, they did patrol their borders. All their borders. There has been an increased presence on our shared border with them. And some report an increase in summer dragons in that area. I wonder why that is, Sadie?"

"Perhaps my parents don't trust us," she said, glancing at the diplomat. "Tell me, Lord Marx, what news do you bring from my father?"

"Well, he has asked for the alliance treaty to be repealed. I think you will find it's just a matter of semantics, really. He cites your conflict of interests, as you have announced that your son Calvin will marry Princess Leticia when he comes of age."

"Interesting how my parents did not even send congratulations on the news of the birth of their first grandchild. You think they would be eager to visit, but yet, nothing," Sadie said, her eyes narrowing.

"Well, they send their congratulations. They have advised me they are glad to hear they have a healthy grandson, and they appreciate the name choice."

"Yes, Calvin Dayia was my grandfather. I've always liked that name," Sadie said, tapping her fingers on the chair.

"I don't think we will repeal the treaty. I'm insulted that Cleon should even suggest it. I have heard vexing news that the summer dragons hide exiles from my lands. Sunrise dragons, living in the caves of Terrek? Is that true, Lord Marx?"

Lord Marx licked his lips. It was true. And he had been advised to not speak of this topic with the King. "Well, I don't know if they live in the caves, sir. I think they might have visited once or twice."

"I see. And may I ask, Lord Marx, did you travel with an entourage?" Nick looked at him dangerously.

"I did. I have several staff members. My secretary, my personal servant, and my intern."

"And where are these people?" Nick asked, his eyes flicking to his bailiff, who stood by the door at attention.

"They are in our quarters, sir. The guest suite upstairs," he said, sweating. Why did the King want to know about his staff? Were they going to be kicked out of Dumara?

"Go get them right away. Pack all your belongings. Bailiff, tell the stables to make their carriage ready."

"Yes, sir!" the bailiff ordered, looking at the diplomat with pity. The King had obviously not liked his message, and he was kicking them out.

The lord nearly ran upstairs, panicking. What had he done wrong? He was just passing along a message. He ordered his staff to pack in haste, and they looked at him in shock, but within ten minutes, they were all back in the throne room, holding their luggage while castle servants packed the trunks onto the top of the carriage.

"Well, now that we are all here, we can continue on with our conversation. Sadie, my dear, I think we need to send a message to your parents. Do you agree?"

"Of course, my dear. A powerful message," she smirked.

"So, which one of these people should die today? I'll let you choose."

"What?" Lord Marx stuttered. "Die? Are you mad?" he said, heat rising to his face. He looked over his staff, and they looked terrified.

"It's a simple choice. I don't think it's fair to kill a member of his staff. They are just hard-working folk, following orders. It's going to have to be Lord Marx, I'm afraid. Plus, I think it will send the message we are looking for, don't you?"

"I agree. Just what we are looking for." Nick stood up and threw his tunic off. They watched in horror as the king unbuckled his pants and let them fall, their mouths hanging open at the scandal of it all.

But they were even more horrified as the King turned into a huge, roaring dragon before their eyes. His red tail flipping back and forth, and his startling blue eyes looking at Lord Marx with pure hunger.

Lord Marx's staff screamed as the dragon lunged forward toward them, lightning fast. With a flip of his head, he snapped his teeth together, inches from Lord Marx.

Lord Marx gave a strangled cry and turned to flee, but he wasn't fast enough for the dragon. With another snap, his teeth closed with delicate precision around Lord Marx's head and neck. With a quick flick of the dragon's long neck, Lord Marx's body separated from his head, and a crimson arch shot across the room, hit the far wall, and then splattered across the marble floor. The body then fell to the staff's feet, spattering their shoes with the life force of their boss. The staff screamed and closed their eyes in terror. The dragon spit out the head, and it landed inches from their feet.

Then the screams died on their lips as they stared in horror at Lord Marx's dead eyes. They took a few steps back and looked at the dragon in terror.

Sadie stepped forward, holding up the astragenica potion. She poured it into the red dragon's mouth, and then watched as her husband transformed back into King Nick of Dumara.

He was naked, of course, and quickly gathered his clothes and dressed. He sat back down on his throne, looking at the staff with disinterest.

"Well, I think I've made my point. Please gather Lord Marx, what remains of him, and return him to King Cleon with a message. My message is this: I do not care. I will do what I want, with whom I want. I WILL release him from the alliance, because it seems pointless. Until the sunrise dragons return to my caves, I will kill every diplomat he sends. Now, leave my sight," Nick said.

The staff just stood there frozen, staring at the body of Lord Marx.

CHAPTER 15

A NEW DAWN

A *MONTH EARLIER:*

The Southern Pearl slipped out of the harbor before dawn, and Mila laid down next to Alex on the narrow bed, her arm across his chest, feeling his regular breaths. She pulled the blanket up over them both and then brushed back his hair. He looked so peaceful and still, and she wondered what he was thinking, so deep in that mind of his.

She closed her eyes and tried to find their connection. She was surprised, after focusing for quite some time, to find it there, tucked into the very back of her consciousness. She reached out to it, but it would not awaken.

Well, she had tried. Maybe tomorrow he would wake up. Or maybe not. She must get some water into him soon. She wondered if he would need to go to the bathroom. She sighed, and then closed her eyes, drifting into sleep as the ship reached the mouth of the harbor. She could feel the ship start to roll as darkness found her.

When she awoke, it was midafternoon. She sat up and looked around her. It all came flooding back, and she looked at Alex, still sleeping peacefully beside her. She shook her head and then got up.

She found her comb in her bag and ran it through her hair. She went out, opened her door, and peeked out on the main deck, thinking there was no time like the present to make her introductions. She needed to find some food for herself and some water for Alex.

"Well, Mila. I see you have awoken. How is your husband?" a voice from behind her spoke, causing her to nearly jump out of her skin.

"Oh hello, Captain Booker. Um, he's not really my husband," Mila confessed; she couldn't stand to lie about something like that. Alex was a married man.

"Please, call me Gideon. Come, talk to me at the wheel. It's a lovely day, and the top deck has some beautiful views."

She considered the captain. He was a tall, lithe man, he looked a little rough, but then again, what captain didn't? He had long black hair, which he wore tied back. He had on knee-length boots, with tan canvas pants tucked into them. He wore a belt, with a short sword at this waist. He wore a white sleeveless shirt tucked into his pants.

She joined him at the wheel. He took it from his first mate, who grinned and stepped aside. "My lady," Norman said, giving her a little bow.

"I trust Normal with my life. He's my partner, in more ways than one," Gideon admitted, throwing him a smile.

Mila looked back and forth between them, and then she realized they were married. They wore matching rings on their left hands. "Ohh," she said, realization dawning. "You're together. As in you love each other."

"Yes, very much. We've been together for nearly twenty years. We met at the bottom of the world, in a hive of villainy called Pelle," Norman said, smiling. "And we've been sailing together ever since."

"So, what I'm trying to say is whatever you tell me, I'll just tell Norman, anyway. But tell me, kid, who is that man who isn't your husband? His name's not Allen, that's for sure," Gideon said, as he paid attention to the waves.

Mila looked at him closely. "My father, Aswin, is the Dragon Keeper of Dumara," she admitted.

Norman whistled, looking at her with a sharp eye. "So that's why he had so much money to throw at us. He's a servant of the King, and I can bet those bags your friend loaded into your cabin weren't just filled with clothes. Those looked awfully heavy."

"He WAS a servant to the King. King Rand is dead, and his son with him," Gideon said, "God rest their souls."

Mila was quiet. She didn't know what to say. On one hand, she felt like she could trust these men, they seemed kind, but was it safe to trust two random sailors she had just met?

"Hey, Gideon, I just had an idea," Norman said, chewing on his thumb.

"Yes, Buttercup?" Gideon asked, raising his eyebrow.

"I don't think Allen is that man's name. You know, I think it might just be Alex. Prince Alex. It's been a while since I glimpsed the Prince, but he fits the specs. Impossibly handsome, blond hair, almost dead."

Mila looked frightened, "Please, sirs. It's not what you think."

Gideon looked at her. "Yeah, it's him all right. For sure. Listen, I don't care who he is. Your father paid me to take you to Norda, and that's where you're going. Just out of curiosity, what's wrong with the man? He seems, well, just about dead."

Mila sighed. "Okay, I guess the jig is up. It is Prince Alex. I am Mila Fletcher, and I am also a Dragon Keeper of Dumara."

"Really? There are two of them? Huh," Norman said, scratching his chin. "Tell me, Mila, we all thought the Prince was dead. How is he not dead?"

"His brother, Nick, poisoned King Rand and Alex, only he failed somehow to give Alex a fatal dose. Believing he was dead, Nick seized power. Only my father and I came to collect the bodies and realized that Alex was still alive. We snuck him out, but he got a terribly high dose of poison, and we don't know when he will wake up."

"So why not just hide him until he wakes up, and then he could take his throne? Dang, all this political intrigue is giving me a headache. I'm glad I'm a ship captain, and I don't have to worry about such things," Gideon said, passing a hand over his eyes.

"Nick has a base of power, and we feared he would find Alex and kill him before he could recover."

"Ah well, I guess it doesn't matter. The ship is headed to Norda, and a fine day it is. I haven't had such nice weather for sailing in I don't know how long. Look how the wind is filling out my lovely new sails!" Gideon said with a smile on his face.

"My uncle cast a spell for good weather," Mila said. "He's the sorcerer."

"Wow, you're really well connected. Did you realize that?" Gideon said. "Now, what can we do to help Alex? He didn't look so great."

"I need to get him to drink some water," Mila admitted.

"That's a good idea. Maybe slap him around a little, that might bring him round," Norman said. "In fact, I'll come with you. I'm interested in our guest."

"Have fun!" Gideon said good-naturedly as he waved goodbye. He was feeling fine, and frankly, quite excited to be on an adventure. He hadn't had this much excitement since running into pirates last spring, when he and Norman had fought side by side, killing them down to the last man, and then pillaging their treasure before sinking the ship. They had had a good spring, living it up in Norda before they had spent it all partying and on boat upgrades, but anyway, they lived day by day, and any day that was filled with excitement was a good day to him.

Norman followed her to the kitchen. "Hey, Cookie. We need a mug of beer for our guest, and maybe some cheese and bread, if you still have any around."

"Beer! I don't know if I should give Alex beer!" Mila exclaimed, horrified.

"Ahh, don't worry, lass. Our water is always a bit stale, being from the hold of the ship. We prefer to drink beer until it runs out. It's a weak brew. It won't get you drunk. If you want something stronger, you'll have to talk to him. They keep the good stuff locked up in their cabin," the cook said, wiping his dirty hands on the front of his filthy apron. He grabbed two metal tankards and filled them from a barrel in the corner.

"Well, you know, Gideon does like a drink or two in the evenings," Norman admitted, picking up the tray of food and a mug of beer.

"Or three. The captain likes his drink, but then again, don't we all?"

"Well, I guess it won't hurt him," Mila said, looking around the ship's kitchen. Unlike the ship's cook, everything was tidy and in its place. Pots hung over the stove, and every plate was put away in the cabinet, held shut with a hook and eye to keep everything from falling out as the ship rocked. The cabinets were filled with tinned provisions. A box of fresh fruit sat on the counter. The cook would use this first, before resorting to the canned stuff.

They made their way back to the room, and Norman sat the tray down on the dresser. The room smelled oddly floral, and he looked around, and then figured it must be some fancy perfume the Prince wore.

Mila sat on the edge of the bed and patted him on the face. His face felt scratchy under her hand, and she could see pale whiskers on his chin. Obviously, it had been days since he had shaved, and she realized she had never seen Alex or his brother with any type of facial hair.

He still didn't move. She leaned over him and spoke directly into his ear. "Alex, this is Mila. You've got to drink, or you'll die of thirst. Come on, wake up enough to take a drink."

He sighed, and it was deep. "I think he heard me!" she said, excitedly, patting his face again.

"Lass, that's no way to wake a man up. Either give him a kiss or give him a good slap."

"I will not hit him!" she exclaimed. She put her arms around him and wrestled him to a sitting position. Norman hurried next to him, putting several pillows behind him, and helping her prop him up.

Now Alex was sitting mostly upright, but he was still stone cold out of it. Mila tried pressing the mug of beer to his lips, but they remained unmoving.

"Alex! You've got to drink," she pleaded, nearly in tears.

"I'm telling you, a slap or a kiss," Norman said, leaning over and staring at the Prince.

"Okay then, don't watch at least," she said, pushing her hair back. Norman rolled his eyes and turned around.

Mila put her lips near Alex's ear, which seemed to work last time. "Alex, this is Mila. You've got to drink. Please, my love. Drink for me," she whispered, and then she planted a kiss on his lips.

They were warm and soft under hers. He moaned, and she nearly jumped with excitement. She quickly held the mug to his lips, and he drank. It was a few gulps at first, and then he stopped.

"DRINK!" she screamed, causing Norman to jump, and Alex started again, and then finished the whole thing.

His eyes flickered open, just for an instant, and a small smile came to his lips, before he slipped back into his comatose state.

Inside her head, she caught one fleeting thought as Alex's consciousness struggled to the surface. "MILA!" and then it was gone again.

"I told you a kiss would work," Norman said, giving her a grin.

"Oh, Norman," Mila said, giving him a stern look, and then she dissolved into laughter, holding her ribs until she couldn't breathe.

———

Gideon had told her it would take them two weeks to reach Norda, and she settled into the trip. She slept with Alex every night, and she noticed he was moving more, and that she was getting more random thoughts. He seemed to know his father was dead, because she kept getting flashes from him, of seeing King Rand sprawled on the floor, and then a flash of Nick's face, laughing cruelly. She was also touched that thoughts of her came to the surface often, and thoughts of his dragonling, the red and gold egg dancing in his mind, with Dahlia behind that.

Her days were spent caring for him, moving his arms and legs so they wouldn't get too weak, changing his bedclothes when he wet himself, and brushing his hair. She felt guilty, because whenever she wanted to get him to drink, she would kiss him.

After she took care of him, she wandered up on the deck, where she would talk to Gideon or Norman. She tried to stay out of the way of the sailors, who were hard at work. She felt them staring at her and realized they didn't see women that often. Gideon promised her that his men would not harm her, they just appreciated seeing a fine woman up on deck. She had blushed at that, the assumption that she was fine.

One day, Norman asked her about her pant suits. "You don't wear dresses, not that I mind. I'm just curious why."

"I don't like them," she shrugged. "And dresses get in the way of me doing my job. Can't ride a dragon in a dress."

"You ride dragons?" Norman said, his eyes going wide.

"Of course. I'm a Dragon Keeper after all," she said.

"Well, Mila. I find I have an all-new respect for you. If I wasn't a taken man, I might have to pursue you, if only for the opportunity that you might take me dragon riding."

"I mean, that sounds amazing," Gideon agreed. "Can I go too?"

Mila laughed, "If we ever have the opportunity, yes, I will take you both dragon riding. But I've heard there aren't any dragons in Norda."

"No, there aren't any dragons. They are prohibited by law. No dragons or any dragon products. So, that little bag of tricks I've seen you with might be illegal."

"Oh," Mila said, worry creasing her face. "It's mostly just herbs and stuff. Although I do have a dragon bone needle in there."

"Why do you need a dragon bone needle?" Gideon asked, curious.

"For sewing together dragon skin, of course. It's the only thing that will pierce it."

"Wow, Mila. You never cease to amaze me," Gideon said, grinning at her.

Seven days into the trip, Mila was sitting on the top deck, enjoying the sun on her face. Her curly brown hair was windblown, but she didn't care. The sun was bright in the sky, and the gulls were chasing the ship. She felt like she was all alone, just a point in the ocean.

Suddenly, she felt a shift and a snap as Alex awoke.

Downstairs, he sat bolt upright and gasped, clutching his chest. His eyes opened, and he looked around wildly. Where was he at? This wasn't the castle. Oh god, his brother had killed their father, for sure, and where was he? He went into panic mode.

Up on the deck, Mila jumped to her feet. "He's awake! He's awake!" she yelled, running down the deck. Gideon looked surprised. How would she know? He followed her down to the cabin.

She threw open the door and collapsed on the bed, crying and kissing him. He looked confused, but returned her kiss, wrapping his arms around her. He was naked, and he didn't know why, or where he was, but he returned her kiss with gusto.

"Mila, where am I? Am I on a boat? Why am I naked? What happened?" he tried to rise, and she pushed him down.

"Easy. You've been out of it for over a week. You're weak, I've done what I can, but you're going to need help walking again."

"Oh, Mila. I had the most terrible dreams," he said, holding his head.

"I'll explain everything, Alex. But first, this is my friend, Captain Gideon Booker. It's his ship, The Southern Pearl that we are on. We are headed for Norda."

Alex looked up at the Captain and offered him his hand. "Pleasure to meet you, sir. Sorry I'm not dressed for the occasion," he said, looking down at the sheet which covered him.

"It's nice to see you up and around, Alex. I'll leave you two alone, and Mila can fill you in. It's quite the story she's shared with us. Later, why don't you join us for dinner? I would love to talk with you more," Gideon said and left the room.

Mila sat with him that afternoon and filled him in from what she knew and what she had seen. He told her he knew the instant he had taken the sip of the tea that it was poisoned. The oily surface had coated his tongue, and he had watched his father fall before losing consciousness himself.

"What of Dahlia, and my son?" he asked, worry crossing his face. He felt guilty, sitting here with Mila in the safety of this ship, while his son and wife were in danger.

"I don't know, Alex. We took the egg and smuggled it out with you. The last I saw it, Sam hid it behind the woodstove. It should stay warm there, but who knows if he will be able hide it very long. And I don't know what became of Dahlia, or Torrid, or any of the other dragons in the caves. I'm assuming they are still safe. I hope my father is safe. He was worried."

"He should have just left me in Dumara! Now what am I supposed to do in Norda? They hate dragons," Alex said, running his hands though his hair, which was now longer than he liked.

"I don't know. He said it was too dangerous in Dumara for you and me, and he worried about sending you to Terrek, thinking that your brother might find you before you could recover or build an army to take back your throne."

Alex shook his head, thinking. "Help me get up. I want to get dressed and go see the sun. If I can't turn into my dragon form, at least I can feel the sun. The light will heal me, even if I'm in human form."

Mila helped him dress, and he laughed as he stumbled around the room, his legs weak. She helped him up to the deck, and the sailors cheered when they saw him. He moved around the deck and then climbed up to the top deck, groaning as he sat on the stool next to the desks that held the maps. He looked at the maps, tracing his finger across the page.

"Good to see you up and around," Norman said from the wheel. "We all thought you were a dead man when we first laid eyes on you."

"I wasn't dead, but I had some hellishly disturbing visions," he said, squinting against the sunlight.

"Maybe I need some of what you had. Sounds like a powerful drug," Norman said. "This weather has been unnaturally good. Mila says her uncle cast a spell."

"Well, it pays to be the niece of the sorcerer," Alex laughed, putting his arm around her. He kissed her forehead.

"You two seem cute together," Normal acknowledged, looking back and forth between them.

Alex cleared his throat and frowned. "I'm actually married," he said, moving away from her.

"Yeah, he is," Mila said, getting quiet.

"Oh, well sorry. That was awkward," Norman said, kicking himself. He hated to see Mila sad. She was a sweet girl, and Alex seemed like a good chap, even if he was married and obviously smitten with his Dragon Keeper.

———

Later that evening, after the sun went down, Mila and Alex joined Norman and Gideon in the Captain's cabin. Cookie came and served them himself. It was a simple meal, of canned beef stew and bread, but Alex devoured two bowls and half a loaf of bread. They watched him eat with fascination.

"I guess he hasn't eaten in a while," Gideon chucked. "So, Alex, now that you've joined the land of the living, what are your plans?"

"I have no idea, to be honest. Perhaps I should try to contact the King of Norda. I've never met Modris before, but my father had. He said he was a fair man."

"One problem, Alex. Modris hates dragons. He is directly related to Mo, you know, the guy who fled across the sea to flee the Dragon King," Gideon said as he opened a bottle of wine and started pouring. "I snitched a case from the hold. No one will mind if our count is off by a case or two."

Alex picked up a glass, and then held it up, touching it to Mila. "Remember the last time we had a drink together?"

"Oh dear, I do. That was embarrassing. I got a little drunk," Mila laughed.

"Cheers!" Norman said, and they all touched glasses and took a drink.

"Well, I have some resources, thanks to Aswin Fletcher. I have enough to buy an army if I can't persuade them to join me," Alex admitted.

"You have that much money? Geeze, Mila, how much money did your father send you with? I should have asked him for more!" Gideon laughed, drained his glass, and pouring another.

"Easy, dear," Norman said, touching his wrist, looking at him with a raised eyebrow.

"Oh, okay," Gideon grumbled, putting his glass down.

"My father sent me with almost his entire life's savings. Well, the gold and silver coin. He knew Dumara banknotes were useless across the sea. I would say, what, 100 pounds of gold?" Mila said, taking a drink of her wine. It was very nice.

"Yeah, about that much," Alex said, looking at Gideon and Norman closely. He trusted them, he didn't know why, and when he had awoken, he realized that some of his visions had revolved around this pair. He would need them in the future. They would be important.

Gideon whistled. "I'm sure you can find some mercenaries in Norda. They work for cheap. I hire them sometimes. If I am taking a load to Fresthav, those icy waters are filled with bloodthirsty pirates. I just don't know if you will find an entire army of mercenaries."

"Well, that seems like a good place to start, and maybe I can talk Modris into helping. Maybe I can make him an offer he can't refuse."

"And what would that be?" Norman asked, curious.

"When I take my throne back, I can guarantee him all the trade I can provide him. Gold, silver, coal, steel, grain. A lot of that goes to Fresthav and Terrek now. Maybe I could guarantee more docks for his ships, favored status, that kind of thing."

"Hmmm, well, like any man, I'm sure King Modris likes money, so he would probably at least listen to your offer."

"I was looking at your map today, Gideon. Where do you think the best place for us to set up is?" Alex asked.

"Well, Norman and I have a little villa. You could stay with us there. But if it's the mercenaries you are looking for, I would suggest Sweetwater. It's on the frontier, and the dwarves live there. They are an insular bunch, but the frontier is rough, filled with bandits and wild animals, and so far from everything that a little coin goes a long way. I hire them from time to time, especially if I'm transporting a load across land from the mines that are rich in that region. I can give you a letter of introduction to Enid. She is the Queen of that rabble."

"Dwarves? I didn't know any of those still existed. I thought they had died out years ago," Alex marveled.

"No, they are still very much in this world. They just are an introverted bunch," Gideon said, draining his glass again and pouring another.

"How about a little music, Buttercup?" he asked Norman. Norman smiled and pulled out a guitar from the nearby closet. He started strumming and played a few songs. Mila was mesmerized and clapped along and sang heartily.

Later, they both stumbled back to the cabin. Alex stripped off his clothes and laid in bed. He turned and looked at her. "Mila, what, are you blushing? You've seen me naked hundreds of times."

"I know, Alex. It's silly, really. I've slept by you all week, but now you are awake," she said.

"Oh, come now. There is only one bed here, and I don't bite, usually," he said, making a chomping motion with his teeth.

She shook her head and then turned away from him, slipping off her clothes. She quickly put on a nightgown and then climbed into bed next to him.

"Mila, I promise. I won't touch you if you don't want me to," he said, raising his hands.

She smiled and snuggled into him. He put his arms around her, closing his eyes as he felt her softness. She was so soft, and he couldn't help to compare her to Dahlia. He had only been with Dahlia one time as a human. The other times, they had mated in dragon form, and it had not been great. It was a chore, and an obligation. He remembered the one night of passion he and Mila had shared, and nothing compared with that.

But he was a married man now, and he wouldn't cheat on his wife, no matter how much he wanted to. He smiled and buried his nose in Mila's hair. It smelled of rainwater and roses, and he realized he probably needed a bath.

Before he knew it, Mila was sleeping in his arms. He kissed her forehead, and her cheeks, so happy for the first time in he didn't know how long.

He knew the odds were stacked against him. His father was dead, his brother had usurped his throne, his own wife and child were dead for all he knew. But he wouldn't give up. He had to at least try. He owed it to his father. And his grandfathers before him.

Soon, he slipped into sleep, and their breathing joined as one in the darkness of the night.

———

The next morning, he arose before dawn, as was his custom. He couldn't fly to greet the sun, but he could do it from the deck of the ship. Mila joined him at the rail as the sailors rose to their morning's tasks.

"Red sky morning, sailors take warning. Storms are coming!" the barrel man shouted from the crow's nest.

Alex smiled and nodded at him, and then sat next to the rail, closing his eyes and feeling the sun on his face. Mila sat next to him, holding his hand, glad that he had come back to her. Together, they watched the sun rise on a new dawn. The sky was the color of blood.

———

Help other readers find Alex and Mila's grand adventure by leaving a rating or review on Amazon or Goodreads!

Subscribe to the author's newsletter for updates, giveaways, and a free prequel novella, *Dane and the Sea Monster*, which tells the story of Gideon and Norman with an adventure on The Southern Pearl. Claim your copy here:

NEXT IN SERIES

The dragon clans of Dumara have set a powerful plot in motion. Can Alex and the dwarves reclaim what is lost? Can they do it before the Dragon God Commath? Find out in the final book of The Dragon Keepers Series. Find it here:

ABOUT THE AUTHOR

Called by some a multi-tasking ninja, Jessica Kemery lives in Crystal Lake, Illinois, where she works a day job so that her dog, Rocky, can live a life of pampered luxury. *The Hobbit* is the first book she read, and she has been searching for dragons ever since. Powered by caffeine and the bare minimum of sleep on a nightly basis, she thinks the world's greatest invention is meal delivery services.

She has a habit of dabbling in all different kinds of fantasy, but all of her stories have strong female characters, sweet romance, action and adventure, deep world building, and maps. Visit https://www.hotmessexpresspublishing.com/works for a complete list of her books. Don't forget to follow her on Facebook, Instagram, Twitter, and TikTok at Author Jessica Kemery.

ABOUT THE AUTHOR